All Passion

DENIED

All Passion DENIED

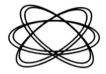

WILLIAM MITCHELL ROSS

To order additional copies of this book, contact:
Xlibris Corporation
1-888-795-4274
www.Xlibris.com
Orders@Xlibris.com
120699

ACKNOWLEDGMENTS

My special thanks to John Baumann, President, Colony Brands, Inc.; Chris and Tyler Soukup, Owners of Baumgartner's Cheese Store and Tavern; Tere Dunlap for her editing advice; and my wife Marilyn, whose continued patience with me during the writing process is remarkable!

GREEN COUNTY, WISCONSIN

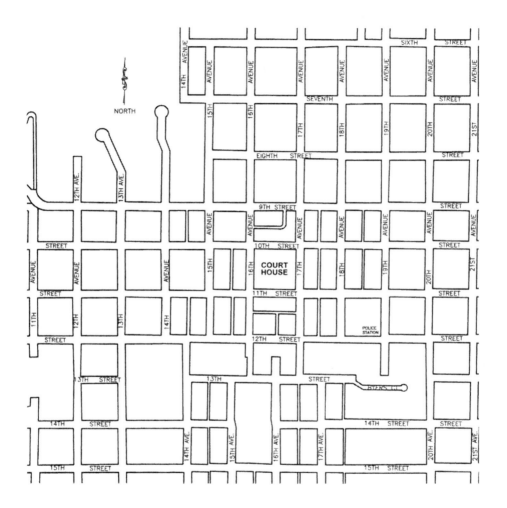

City of Monroe

DOWNTOWN AREA

CHAPTER 1

Darkening ominous storm clouds gathered in the sky and raced toward the city of Monroe, pushed by straight-line force winds. The once clear blue skies had collapsed under the weight of the storm. An enormous thunderstorm, laced with luminous lightning, was fast developing west of the Mississippi River. The ferocity of the raging storm was venting its anger on the earth below.

The local radio station had advised all citizens to stay in their homes for the night. Emergency broadcasts warning of extreme weather had been going out over the air waves all afternoon. The weather moving in was very severe, and the station warned that anyone venturing out would be at the risk of their own peril. It was reported that a weather event of this magnitude happens only every ten years and had to be respected. The threat of possible tornadoes and hail was always a concern. To the old timers, this was only another old-fashioned Midwest summer storm. But their memories also reminded them of the havoc and devastation brought about by the 1965 Palm Sunday tornado that cut a devastating path through the west side of the city just two years before.

During the twilight of darkness on this mid-June night, the storm reached Monroe. The muffled roar of the racing wind grew louder and louder. As the storm moved in, trees swayed violently. It was like some unseen giant hand fiercely shaking the branches. Branches and twigs were flying everywhere. The sudden cracking sound of a tree breaking in half echoed through the noise and chaos.

A few people stood looking out the windows of their houses at the raging storm. They were waiting and listening for that fateful wailing siren announcing the threat of a tornado. The terrifying sight of a snake-like funnel cloud rapidly descending to earth had been etched into their minds since childhood. They were all anxious now, waiting and watching.

The streets were deserted. No one was out braving the wind and rain. Only abandoned cars were parked on the wind-swept streets. Street lights flickered in the din, giving the city a surreal look. Lightning flashes continually lit up the sky, followed by clashing thunder. The hard-driving rain and hail came down in torrents. Rivers of water were soon running down the streets, causing whirlpools of foamy water at stressed-out storm sewers. The occasional snapping sound of old oak trees added to the commotion.

Then, suddenly, the lone figure of a man got out of his car. How long had he been sitting there? Was he waiting out the storm? He was wearing a black waxed weather-proof trench coat and a Stetson all-weather hat. The hat was pulled down tightly around his face as he fought off the fierce winds and stinging rain. As he walked, he lowered his head against the ferocity of the wind-driven rain.

He was parked on Lincoln Avenue, a street parallel to the Country Club. A row of homes separated the street from the hedgerow bordering the county club. He slowly made his way to an easement between two houses, a path used as a walking entrance onto the club property—mostly by kids as a short cut.

When he got to the entrance, he paused and looked back in the direction of his car for some moments. He hesitated, as if undecided about what to do next. Then he turned toward the entrance and pressed on against the wind.

Once through the hedgerow, he could clearly see the parking lot, club house and swimming pool. In the distance, he could see a couple of the golf course greens.

He then made his way slowly and carefully along the edge of the boxwood hedgerow shielding his body from the wind and rain. His well-worn cowboy boots were totally soaked, but he didn't seem to notice. The wind and rain battered him ferociously as he inched his way forward walking beside the parking lot.

The barrier hedge was approximately four feet from the edge of the asphalt. He was desperately trying to shield himself from the storm using the eight-foot hedge as protection.

He worked his way toward the only car in the parking lot—a silver BMW. When he got to the car, he stopped and backed his five-foot, ten-inch frame up against the hedge.

Once he was settled in, this mysterious man seemed indifferent to the storm raging around him. He strained to look across the parking lot into the bar area of the club house. As he stared at the building, the incessant rain droplets dripped off the bill of his hat. During the lightning flashes, he could see the golf course's number nine green. The flag on the green was fluttering helplessly in the wind. He stood very still as the hedge whipped back and forth above his head, fighting off the wind.

His hands were buried deep into the depths of his trench coat. In his right pocket, he was fondling the handle of a gun. The man was armed with a gun, resentment and anger. He could feel the cold steel of death as his finger stroked the barrel. The gun was a Smith and Wesson .38 Special. He felt very calm as he cradled the gun in his hand. He was thinking about what he was going to do next, but until then, he was determined to be patient and wait.

The two gentlemen in the brightly lit bar were unaware of the steely eyes focused on them from the outside parking lot. Dr. George Andrew Buckle, a cardiac surgeon at the Monroe Regional Medical Center, was on his third whisky and water. He was a thin, tall and angular man. He had short brown hair, dark eyes and a long nose.

Buckle was seated on a black leather barstool. Across the bar were four beer towers featuring the local brews from the Leuenberger Brewing Co. Brian, the bartender, had placed a bowl of pretzels and peanuts next to his drink. He slowly sipped his drink and impatiently looked at his watch. He listened to the peaceful, classical music playing in the lounge area, which contrasted the raging storm outside.

Buckle had graduated with honors from St. Andrews Medical School in Oxford, England. Upon graduation, he immediately accepted a job at Boston General Hospital in Massachusetts. After a few years, he left there and was now in Monroe. He fancied himself the crown jewel of surgeons at the medical center and had an enormous ego to accompany his self-importance.

He was waiting for his wife, Dr. Ingrid Lindquist, a psychiatrist who also worked at the medical center. She told him earlier that day that she would meet him at the county club for drinks when she finished with her last patient. She was late, and Buckle was feeling the effects of the whisky.

"Where the hell is she?" he asked Brian, who was cleaning up the bar area and getting ready to close up and go home. Buckle was the only remaining customer, which irritated Brian. Everyone else had left early due to the storm warnings. He had only been working at the club for a year, but the reputation of the arrogant doctor was well known. His arrogance and self-serving attitude were tolerated by the staff, because he was a very big tipper. They had learned to humor him and ignored the insults.

"Maybe the storm is causing her some problems," Brian suggested.

"You call this a storm!" Buckle suddenly bellowed. "It doesn't even measure up to the great storms that we had in England when I was a boy. Those were hellish storms, and I lived through a lot of them. They tore the roofs off buildings and killed people. Those horrific storms scared the old people very badly. As they hid from the storm's wrath in their homes, the buildings would rattle and shake in gale force winds that could reach seventy-five knots! Now, those were the storms worth talking about!" Buckle picked up his glass and toasted the storm raging outside. He threw back his head and drained the remaining liquid from his glass.

"Give me another drink," he demanded. Then he eased his six-foot-two frame off his bar stool and headed for the gents. In the bar area, there were ten round black tables, and each one of them had four black ornate chairs. He staggered unevenly as he made his way to the green felted pool table next to the restrooms. The women's was on the left and the men's on the right.

Brian watched him disappear into the bathroom and poured the doctor another drink.

The phone rang and Brian answered it on the second ring. The line had static in it. The voice on the other end was Buckle's wife. He laid the phone down on the bar and headed for the gents. Before he got there, the door swung open and Buckle emerged. "Your wife is on the phone," he said.

Buckle bumped into a chair as he made his way to the phone and picked it up rubbing his leg with his left hand.

"Where the hell are you?" he roared into the receiver. He listened for a few moments, and then told her that waiting for her was a real inconvenience for him. She said something else, and Buckle told her to piss off and slammed down the receiver. "Damn impertinent woman!"

Buckle settled back onto his bar stool and looked out the window. "I will remember this treacherous night because of the bruise on my leg," he told Brian. Brian ignored him and took a sip from his fountain soda.

Lightning flashed and the sound of thunder soon followed. He looked back at Brian. "Do you know how far away that lightning was? Of course not," he said answering his own question. "If you count the seconds between the lightning and the clap of thunder and divide by five, then you will know how many miles away it was," he said with authority. Brian absently nodded. Buckle picked up his drink and took a sip. "Damn fine whisky."

"Do you know what Ingrid told me? She is my Swedish wife if you didn't know," Buckle asked. Brian shrugged.

"She told me that, when she went to the parking lot at the medical center tonight, a tree had been uprooted in the wind and crashed onto her car. She then had a friend take her home. Do you think that she could have called me first? Oh no! She had to go home, because she thought the damn dog might be scared. Can you believe that? She chose the damned dog over me!" He took another sip of his whisky.

"I think you should be going home yourself doctor. The storm seems to be getting worse," Brian said.

Buckle laughed. "Brian, if you were an educated man, you would know that severe thunderstorms are about fifteen miles in diameter and last an average of thirty to forty-five minutes. In my estimation, this puny little rain event is almost over. But you are right, I should be heading out."

"Thank God," Brian thought.

Buckle finished his drink, stood up and steadied himself. Brian retrieved the doctor's rain coat from the coat tree rack and handed it to him. "Thanks Brian," he said as he slipped on the coat. He reached into his pants pocket and took a twenty-dollar bill from his money clip and handed it to him. "Keep the change," he said. He then headed toward the exit door that led to the parking lot.

When Buckle opened the door, Brian could see the rain was letting up. "I'll be damned," he said to himself. After Buckle left, he hastily locked the frosted-etched glass door. He turned off the bar lights, put on his rain jacket and hastily left out the rear exit door on the opposite side of the bar, locking the door behind him.

Buckle made his way unevenly to his car, swaying a little in the dying winds that blew against him. He was almost to his car when a flash of lightning illuminated a figure walking toward him. Buckle laughed. "What the hell? Is this a cowboy I see out in this weather?" he shouted and laughed again above the din. The figure stopped about five feet from him and remained silent. Suddenly, three shots rang out in the stormy night.

Instantly, Buckle was felled. As he lay on the pavement next to his BMW, his hand reached over and touched his chest; his red, warm, life-giving blood flowed out of him toward the cold, wet, dark asphalt. He lost consciousness.

The storm surged again, suddenly and furiously, lashing out with deafening thunder and lightning bolts, crying out in anguish at the sight of this murder by frontier justice.

CHAPTER 2

Early Friday morning Monroe Police Chief Brandon Johns was relaxing at his kitchen table, drinking coffee. His wife, Beth, was preparing eggs and bacon for breakfast. The sun was shining in brightly through their kitchen window. The storm last night was one for the memory books. He had already surveyed the outside of his house and yard for damage and, other than some downed tree branches and twigs, saw no problems. Even the old elm tree in the front yard survived the fierce winds.

The night before, he had gone home early from work, anticipating the severity of the storm. The kids were staying at their grandparents' farm in Juda—a short drive to the east of Monroe. Johns thought it a better idea to wait out the storm with Beth since she was alone. If an emergency call came in to the P.D., he could easily be reached.

As the storm raged outside, he and Beth sat on their living room sofa peering out their over-sized bay window. She had turned the lights down low as they cuddled together. The lightning flashes and thunder rolls were awesome. Beth would jump a little at the sound of the thunder and lightning and snuggle even closer to the chief. He didn't mind and was enjoying the closeness with his arms secured around her. He could smell the scent of her shampoo and found it intoxicating. Their busy work schedules and raising their hyper boys had made quiet moments like this impossible. Thank God for grandparents, he mused.

The howling winds became more intense and surrounded the house. When the lights began to flicker, Beth suggested candles and got them ready. The chief asked if they had any wine. She retrieved a bottle of Chablis and two stemmed glasses. He popped the cork and poured the clear liquid into the glasses. They toasted the storm and settled in again.

At approximately seven thirty, the lights went out. Lightning flashes lit up the living room as Beth lit the candles. As the chief refilled their glasses, he saw Beth's face in the soft glow of the candle light. She was radiant and her wry smile got his attention. She was enjoying the moment. For an instant, time stopped for him. She looked beautiful. He couldn't remember the last time he felt a moment like this one. He felt very much in love.

He grabbed her hand and gently squeezed it. Beth snuggled in closer and put her hand on his thigh. He kissed her and he instantly felt an irresistible desire. In a heartbeat, they were tightly inter-twined around one another. Beth grabbed the candle as they hastily made their way to the bedroom. Making love to the sound of the raging storm outside greatly added to their pleasure. Afterwards, they both fell into a satisfying deep sleep.

The next morning the memory of her sweet kisses still lingered. As the familiar smell of the bacon filled the kitchen, the phone rang. The chief looked at Beth and she smiled. "Go answer it," she said.

Johns picked up the phone, and didn't say anything for a few moments. Then he said, "Okay" and hung up.

"Do you have time for breakfast?" Beth asked.

"Yes, and then I have to go. A body was discovered in the parking lot of the Country Club this morning." He finished his breakfast, kissed Beth goodbye and backed his unmarked police car out of his driveway.

Johns pulled into the Country Club parking lot at eight fifteen, and immediately saw a small crowd of people standing near the black-and-white patrol cars. He pulled up next to the crowd and exited his car. Greetings of "Hello, Chief" rang out from the crowd as he made his way to the body. The area was secured with yellow crime scene tape located next to a silver-colored BMW.

Police Captain Russ Sigenthaler turned and watched him approach. "We've already called Dr. Ken Anderson," he said.

Johns went over to the body and stared at it. Then Sigenthaler filled him in. Fritz Figi, a summer groundskeeper employee of the county club, reported to work early to check out any storm damage. He eventually made his way to the parking lot and spotted the body lying next to the Silver BMW. His first thought was that the person had been struck by lightning. But after closer examination, he wasn't so sure and immediately called the police. After the patrol cars arrived, curious local citizens made their way to the parking lot.

They had been out surveying storm damage at their homes when they saw the patrol cars speed by. Johns looked back at the crowd of onlookers and shook his head. He was sure that the speculation and local gossip was at a fever pitch.

Police Officer Kennickson joined the twosome, and he and Sigenthaler filled the chief in on what they had done so far. They had ascertained that the victim was indeed dead, so they didn't need to call an emergency vehicle. Instead, Kennickson put in the call to Dr. Ken, the medical examiner, to come and officially confirm that the victim was dead. Only then could the body be removed. He then called Albert Swenson, the owner of a photography studio on the square, who was on call to be a crime scene photographer when needed.

While all this was going on, Sigenthaler interviewed the folks in the crowd, but no one had seen or heard anything—only the patrol cars speeding past their houses. By keeping the crowd at a distance, the crime scene was preserved, except for turning the body over to examine it. The crowd was nosily talking to one another about never seeing a dead body before. The sight of the corpse had them mesmerized.

As the officers were talking, Dr. Ken and Swenson arrived at the same time. Sigenthaler took Swenson to the body. He began taking pictures from every angle to clearly show the size and distance of every detail.

"Good morning, Chief," Dr. Ken began, "Couldn't ask for a better day after last night."

Johns looked at him. "Not a good day for him," he said and pointed to the corpse.

Dr. Ken laughed. "I suppose not."

Dr. Ken started a running dialog, talking to no one in particular. "Tall thin man in a raincoat; khaki pants; no hat; blue dress shirt; no tie; wearing Francesco Benigno black leather shoes; drinks too much, probably whiskey and water."

Chief Johns stared at him, "Say what?" Dr. Ken ignored him. They stood in silence as Swenson finished taking pictures. Finally, satisfied he had all the pictures he needed, Swenson told the chief he was finished.

Swenson left, and Dr. Ken moved in to examine the body. After a brief examination, he stood up. "Okay. Dr. Buckle is officially dead. He died from three gunshot wounds to the chest area. No burn marks, so I would say that the shots were fired some distance from the victim. He bled out on the pavement. I would estimate the time of death to be from seven to ten last night. And if you are interested, I would say he was murdered. After I remove the bullets back at the lab, you may pick them up." Then he handed the chief Buckle's wallet and money clip.

"Drinks whiskey and water?" Johns asked.

"He lives near me on 'Pill Hill,' and I have been to a few of his wife's candlelight dinner parties," Dr. Ken laughed. He often referred to his banter with Johns as emotional anesthesia.

Officer Kennickson approached them as they stared at the body being put into a plastic bag and loaded into the awaiting ambulance.

"We ran the tags, Chief, and the car is registered to a Doctor George Andrew Buckle," he said. "He lives here in Monroe in a pretty ritzy neighborhood, according to the address."

"Pill Hill, according to the Dr. Ken," Johns said. Dr. Ken smiled and walked back to his car.

Due to the heavy rains the previous night, no other information could be ascertained from the crime scene. According to the officers, no foot prints or other evidence was visible. Sigenthaler told the chief that he was going to interview the bartender and canvass the neighborhood for anyone who might have seen anything of importance last night. The bartender was probably the last person to see him alive.

Johns gave Sigenthaler the wallet and gold-plated money clip to bag up. The clip had five twenty-dollar bills in it. "I don't think robbery was the motive," he said.

He told the officers to file a very detailed and complete report on the homicide. They must keep notes on everything including all relevant times, starting from when they first arrived on the scene. They needed to list all the people at the crime scene and to make a detailed report on the conditions of the crime scene as they found it.

After he finished his directives, Johns walked with Sigenthaler along the parking lot to the entrance of the club property through the hedgerow. Kennickson had wandered over to the crowd of onlookers.

Johns noticed a slight limp in Sigenthaler's gait due to an injury he had received chasing a juvenile over a fence. "Does your leg still bother you?" he asked.

"There isn't any pain if that's what you mean. I am hoping that the limp will work itself out."

They stood staring at the club entrance in the hedgerow. Johns didn't say anything; Sigenthaler knew what he was thinking. This is probably where the murderer came through last night. They didn't see any footprints in the grass. Maybe Kennickson would have better luck.

As they returned to the police cars, Johns told Sigenthaler that he was going back to the police station and call Detective Samantha Gates. Since he needed to go to a police conference in Washington, D.C., he told him that Gates would initially be handling the investigation with his help. Johns also said he wanted them both to go and break the news to Dr. Buckle's wife. He felt Sam's presence would help soften the news.

"Every crime scene has a story to tell, and I want to know what this one says," Johns said as he jumped into his police car and followed the ambulance out of the parking lot.

Captain Sigenthaler walked over to Kennickson. "Chief seems to be in a pretty good mood this morning considering what had just happened. He even had a smile on his face."

"That will change after Roger Nussbaum contacts him!" Kennickson replied. They both laughed.

CHAPTER 3

Detective Samantha Gates had arrived at her second floor apartment in Monroe at eight thirty that Friday morning. She was resting in her overstuffed favorite chair. She could hear the early morning birds chirping away though her partially opened sliding glass door, and recognized the sound of a cardinal.

Her slim five-foot, ten-inch frame fit the chair perfectly. She was wearing a light blue cotton blouse and tan slacks. The shoes she had been wearing were kicked off, exposing her bare feet. She held a fresh cup of steaming black coffee in her hand as she stared out her living room window.

As of late, things had been pretty slow at the police department. After her last case of murder in Monroe, the dull routine of police work had kicked in. Tracking down a couple of petty thefts and interviewing the victims kept her busy, but not invigorated. She planned to report to work about nine thirty to catch up on any storm stories that came into the police department from last night.

Sam had spent the night in Madison with her good friend Janet Finley. The bad weather reports about the approaching storm had been broadcasted on the news all day, so Janet suggested that she wait out the storm in Madison. Sam agreed, and the ride back to Monroe this morning had been sunny and pleasant. Once she arrived in Monroe, she saw city employees and their trucks cleaning up the tree branches and twigs. She passed by two houses that had felled trees in their yards. Another house had an elm tree leaning against the side of the house. Janet was right!

Last fall, while solving a murder case, Sam received a severe blow to the back of her head that gave her a concussion. She went on emergency medical leave from the police department. During her slow recovery period, she experienced some memory problems that were being treated in Madison. The official diagnosis given to Sam was stress and exhaustion.

The good news was that after four months she was able to return to work. However, she was still receiving outpatient treatment just to insure of a full recovery. Her headaches were gone and her memory was much improved. But Chief Johns still allowed her extra time off when she felt like she needed it. She appreciated the light duty she was given. It allowed her stay in touch with the other police officers and her work.

During her treatment and time off, Sam was able to move her mother, Sharon Gates, to the Parkview Nursing Home in Monroe. Her mother had previously lived in Silver Bay, Wisconsin, located two hours east of Monroe in Racine County. After the murder of her husband Earl, a police officer, Sharon had become clinically depressed and unable to take care of herself. Her life had compressed itself into smaller and smaller circles, and she needed supervised care.

Sam's older brother, Phil, suffered from addictions and had abandoned the family. Sam had taken on the sole responsibilities as the caregiver for her mom.

Her dad, Earl Gates, had been a police officer in the Silver Bay Police Department. When Sam was sixteen, he was shot and killed during a routine nocturnal traffic stop. His abruptly shortened life and tragic death propelled the family into the chaos of shock, sadness and grief. Rivers of tears flowed from Sam and her mother. The two suspects were never caught, and the case eventually became a cold one.

At a young age, Sam was devastated. She adored and loved her dad, and she had fanaticized about him walking her down the aisle at her wedding. He would have been a wonderful grandparent to her children.

In a sense, there were two deaths that fateful night. Her hopes and dreams were shattered, and her life became one of obsession to become a police officer. Her passion was to find the killers and bring them to justice.

From her desk at the Monroe Police Department, Sam would call Police Chief Cal Thompson at the Silver Bay Police Department for any updates on Earl's case. But the answer was always the same, "We will call you if anything turns up."

Earl's death had galvanized Sam's resolve to become a police officer, and she made it her life's work, passion and mission to apprehend the killers. In her quiet reflective moments, Earl was still very much alive to her. He continued to occupy Sam's thoughts the same way he did when he was alive.

It was as if he was on a journey somewhere waiting for the news. When she visited his grave, she told him that she would find the killers so he could rest in peace. That graveside promise tormented her. The sad truth that she learned to live with was that death wasn't just for the old but is there from the beginning.

Being a woman detective in the police department was a novelty, and she had a very tough time of it. She always had to prove how tough she was and had to over achieve on any assignment given to her. Her tenaciousness in solving a murder case last fall had given her the measure of respect she needed within the department. Even though she felt she was better accepted, being the outlier in a testosterone—driven job had its challenges.

During her treatments for her memory gaps at St. Mary's Hospital, Sam stayed overnight with Janet, her old college roommate on Mifflin Street. After starting her job at the Monroe police department, she had reconnected with Janet to help jump start her social life. Sam didn't feel comfortable dating anyone in Monroe, knowing the culture and gossip of small towns.

Janet's circle of friends consisted of holdovers from their college days, and Sam felt very comfortable being around them. The group also offered new opportunities to meet guys. The problem Sam encountered was her profession. Being a police detective seemed to attract the wrong type of guys. Initially, they were pleasant enough, but ultimately they wanted to know about cases that she had worked on, especially the ones concerning sex crimes. When Sam refused to discuss her work, she disappointed them to the extent that they would generally fade away.

She confided in Janet that she really wanted a relationship to keep more balance in her life. She was looking for a man to love and who would love her back. Someone she could trust. Janet's response was "Good luck with that!"

Then by happenstance, she met someone. During one of her sessions with the memory therapist, she noticed a young man in his early thirties working in the same area of the hospital. She found out that his name was Drew Nelson. He was six feet one with a round face that featured a nose that looked like it had been broken. His flaming red hair made him stand out in a crowd. He had been a high school quarterback and still had an athlete's physique.

After the usual smiles and greetings in the hallways, Sam asked him to share a cup of coffee with her in the hospital cafeteria. She instantly discovered that he was a very nice guy. He asked non-intrusive questions about her, which made her very comfortable. In his own relaxed way, he made her feel special.

He worked as a physical therapist, and she liked the easy manner in which he described his work. She also found out that he wasn't dating anyone. He wasn't even put off by the question. Another thing she liked was that he wasn't wrapped up in all the macho ego crap that athletes generally carry around with them. His ability to be a good listener and be interested in her was refreshing. When Sam told him she was a police detective, it didn't alarm him. In fact, he complemented her for her courage to pursue a police career. He also told her she was the first female police detective he had ever met. They both laughed.

Janet was excited Sam had met someone she liked, but cautioned her about two things. The first caution was that Sam was thirty-three years old, and Drew was thirty-one. Not a huge difference in age, but a concern. And secondly, when Sam got involved in a case, it became a twenty-four/seven job for her, leaving precious little time for anything else. Sam totally agreed with her second point. If her work interfered with her dating Drew, she would have to adjust her work schedule. But on some level, her inner voice was saying this adjustment could be a concern. Easier said than done, she thought.

Over the next couple of months, Sam's trips to Madison became more frequent because of Drew. Janet offered up her apartment as a love nest, and everything went along very well. She was happy for the routine at Monroe's PD. It allowed her more time for her therapy and time with Drew. Her doctor's confident prognosis was for a one-hundred percent chance for a total recovery.

Sam felt her life was heading in a positive direction, except for one thing. It was like a dark cloud hovering over her. She felt a sense of guilt over three deaths: her father's murder was unsolved, the suicide of a fellow police officer at the Silver Bay Police Department and a recent death in Monroe. She had contacted Pastor Carl Peterson from the First Christian Church of Monroe for counseling. Perhaps she could exorcise the demons that troubled her with the good pastor's care. At any rate, that was her hope.

For the time being, dating Drew was great. She learned that he had a good sense of humor and was very thoughtful. He seemed to sense when something was troubling her and would surprise her with a fresh bouquet of colorful flowers. The flowers and his thoughtfulness immediately cheered her up.

Janet's apartment was on the second floor facing Mifflin Street. An elderly woman in her eighties lived in the apartment below Janet's. Ruth Erickson usually sat in her reclining rocker all day with her blinds wide open watching television. The comings and goings of the other residents in the apartment building never went unnoticed. Over the years she had brief conversations with Janet but never got to know her. Janet was just another one of the many faces of people who moved in and moved out. The only constant was Ruth who had lived there for twenty years.

Whenever Drew showed up at apartment building, she would carefully lift herself up out of her chair and grab her cane and stand next to the window. She figured out that when the tall girl was there Drew seemed to be not far behind. She could also hear footsteps in the apartment above her when she turned down the television.

Sometimes, she would venture outside and stare up at the apartment above hers. She really didn't know the other women who visited above her, but her curiosity was killing her. Her imagination had been running wild ever since Sam and Drew showed up at Janet's apartment. Whatever was happening above her, Ruth just knew that it had to be sinful! She even thought about reporting it to management!

Ruth had a disapproving scowl on her face as she kept her vigilance. Like the troll under the bridge, she monitored this sinful activity with keen interest. Sometimes, as Drew was leaving, he would pause on the sidewalk, turn and wave to her. The old troll ignored him. Then one afternoon as he was leaving, Drew walked over to her sliding glass door, which was open. He smiled and waved to her and wished her a nice day. Ruth went nuts! She slowly raised her arm with her middle finger extended upward. Sam and Drew laughed themselves silly when retelling this story to their friends.

The sudden ringing of the telephone startled Sam and brought her thoughts back to Monroe. The voice on the other end was Chief Johns. He briefly filled her in on the murder of Dr. Buckle and requested that she and Captain Sigenthaler visit the wife to break the news. She agreed to meet at the PD at ten. She and Sigenthaler could then ride over together. As she put the receiver down, Sam felt a familiar rush of adrenaline in her body.

CHAPTER 4

Dr. Ingrid Lindquist was snuggled in under the covers of her four-posted antique bed that Friday. It was seven thirty, and the morning sun was shining brightly through her bedroom window. When she opened her eyes she saw her dog, Guinevere, snuggled beside her. Guinevere looked up and wagged her tail, obviously ready to get up and start the day. Ingrid was happy today was her day off.

She couldn't get to sleep until after midnight the night before. The noisy storm, her car being smashed by a tree, a scared dog and a bastard for a husband kept her mind whirling until she finally fell asleep, mostly from exhaustion. But now she was fully awake.

Ingrid jumped out of bed and shook her head in disgust as she went to the bathroom to freshen up. She quickly surmised that her husband hadn't come home last night. Just to be sure, she put on a white terry cloth bathrobe over her silk pajamas. Then she slipped on a pair of slippers and made a quick survey of the house with Guinevere at her heels.

They lived in an oversized two-story, red brick, Colonial-style house that had three thousand square feet of living space. Ten years earlier, a doctor from Virginia had built the house. He didn't seem to care that he was living a Swiss community. He told the builder he was homesick and wanted a house that reminded him of Virginia. The house was pricy to build with all the pillars, vaulted ceilings and a big front porch, but the doctor paid cash. He only lived there four years before taking another job offer from a hospital in Richmond, Virginia.

A second doctor bought the house at a reduced price after it was on the market for more than a year. It was the only house of its kind in Monroe. All the houses in the Pill Hill area were nice and conformed to the neighborhood, but this one stood out like something leftover from a movie set.

After that doctor got a job at the Mayo Clinic and moved to Rochester, Minnesota, Dr. Buckle bought the house. It wasn't Dr. Lindquist's first choice, but it was available and their move to Monroe was rather sudden.

After ten minutes of searching the house and finding an empty garage, Ingrid finished up her walking tour in the kitchen. She was right, of course. Her husband didn't come home last night, and God only knew whose bed he found comfort in during the storm. Guinevere started to whine, so she let her out into the backyard. The dog scampered through the open doorway, and then she turned to put on a pot of coffee to brew with freshly ground Swedish Gevalia Kaffe beans.

Ingrid took a quick shower and, since today was her day off from the hospital, dressed in blue jeans, a flowered cotton yellow shirt. She slipped her bare feet into a pair of soft leather loafers. With her hair still damp, she headed back to the kitchen and poured herself a cup of coffee. It tasted delicious. The steaming coffee was comfort food for her when she was feeling low. She looked out the window and saw Guinevere running around exercising her legs.

Ingrid grabbed her cup of coffee and joined the dog in the backyard. Setting the cup on a wrought iron deck table, she picked up a stick and threw it as far as she could. Immediately, Guinevere chased it down and returned it to her. She threw it again several times to the dog's delight. Then, Ingrid, with coffee cup in hand, and Guinevere causally made their way around the fenced yard together, looking for storm damage.

Ingrid Lindquist was born and raised in Stockholm, Sweden. A favorite among her classmates, she was a very bright and cheerful student and had a natural talent for her studies. Her lifelong dream was to be a psychiatrist just like her aunt, Lill-Marta Nilsson. Through hard work, persistence and encouragement from her aunt, she earned her degree. It was the happiest day of her life.

Her first job after university had an international sense of adventure to it. She accepted a job at Boston General Hospital in Massachusetts. Going to America was a dream come true for her. She couldn't believe her good luck. Her family was very excited and made frequent trips to the United States to visit her and explore the wonders of America. They had distant relatives in Chicago, so that was a frequent destination. Ingrid enjoyed these visits, and she felt comfortable around them. These Swedish ancestors were a reminder of the mass emigration from Sweden to America in the 1800s. Their stories of hardship and perseverance inspired her, and a sense of connectedness to them and Sweden touched her soul.

At Boston General she met Dr. George Andrew Buckle. He was a brilliant heart surgeon from the UK. He was touted as a rising star by his colleagues in the medical profession. He was thirty-five; she had just turned thirty. He had a reputation as a ladies man, but Ingrid was in love with him and ignored the gossip. They married a year later.

Things were going along swimmingly in their marriage and in their careers, until he was profiled in a prestigious medical journal for his brilliant work as a heart surgeon. George Andrew Buckle became an overnight celebrity. His over-the-top ego got even bigger as he became totally consumed with his new status. With all the attention he was getting, his womanizing habits re-surfaced, leaving his wife in the abyss of embarrassment and shame. Ingrid found herself living in the long shadow of her husband. She was now expected to abandon her own career responsibilities whenever he needed her for his speaking engagements or entertaining snobbish friends.

Dr. Buckle was soaring high in his career and new-found celebrity status. He demanded pay raises and perks at Boston General. His social drinking got out of control. He was driving Ingrid crazy. Then suddenly, like Icarus, his world came crashing down.

The realization of her shaky marriage to Buckle became very clear to her after an incident at hospital. One of Buckle's heart patients died during an operation. The family sued the hospital for damages. What complicated things was the fact that Buckle performed the surgery under the influence of alcohol. One of the surgical nurses thought she smelled booze on the doctor, but she couldn't prove it. The investigation got very messy, and the hospital settled out of court.

Then things got worse. Buckle sexually assaulted a nurse at a hospital party. He was drunk at the time and denied any knowledge of the incident. The nurse didn't have a strong case against him, so she dropped the charges. But after that incident, the hospital had had enough of Dr. Buckle and quietly gave him notice. He wanted to go the Mayo Clinic in Minnesota, but he couldn't get the references he needed. As a compromise, he settled for a job at the Monroe Regional Medical Center with outstanding references and glowing praise for his work at Boston General. The Hospital Administrator at the Monroe Regional Medical Center, Chester Hadden, was instantly elevated to the status of brilliancy and given much praise for bringing such a prominent heart surgeon to the hospital.

After all the drama in Boston and the relocation, Ingrid's marriage very rapidly fell apart. Buckle's drinking continued to be a problem and his relationship with his wife became distant. When they were courting, Ingrid saw her husband as funny, intelligent and charmingly sarcastic. Now all that had changed. "When you think you are in love, it can become an illusion with terrible consequences. I am a professional psychiatrist, and I should have known better!" she lamented.

She was now living out those consequences. Even their love making had taken a bizarre twist. He would throw her down on the bed and hold her down during sex. He found this to be very exciting. She thought it disgusting.

The frustration of the marriage was getting to her. She wasn't sleeping well at night—in fact, she couldn't remember the last time she had a good, sound sleep. Dr. Ingrid Lindquist diagnosed herself as having physiological and psychological health problems. She decided to follow the advice she had given a number of her clients: Get a pet. She told them pets can be a source of love, affection and companionship. Now she was going to try the advice on herself.

She actively researched the kind of pet that she felt best suited her and settled on a Welsh Springer Spaniel. She was able to locate a puppy in Chicago and traveled there by herself to pick it up. Buckle thought the whole idea of a pet was ridiculous and refused to take any part in it. To her surprise, the puppy came with a remarkable list of pedigrees, and the ancestral line was impressive. She didn't tell Buckle what she paid for the adorable puppy, but the cost was as impressive as the pedigree.

She named the puppy Guinevere, after King Arthur's wife in Camelot, her favorite story as a child. Buckle made fun of the new puppy and called it 'Welshie' just to irritate her. She ignored him.

The new puppy did wonders for Ingrid. She started feeling better about herself right away. She took it for walks around the neighborhood and quickly met her neighbors. She also enjoyed the exercise. Guinevere was always excited and glad to see her when she got home from work. All the attention and petting immediately relaxed her. It was nice to have someone love you, even if it was a dog.

Back in the kitchen, Ingrid filled Guinevere's food dish and gave her fresh water. She then poured herself a bowl of granola cereal and poured a glass of orange juice. She sat down at the kitchen table to enjoy her breakfast. She guessed Buckle would come wandering in sometime before noon and ignore her like all the other times.

The phone suddenly rang and interrupted her thoughts. She answered it on the second ring, thinking it was Buckle. It was the police wanting to come over to see her. They didn't give a reason for the visit. Probably to fill out a report on my smashed car, she thought.

Detective Gates and Captain Sigenthaler sat in a squad car outside of the Lindquist-Buckle house just before ten a.m. "Do you think we should have told her over the phone?" Sigenthaler asked.

"No, I don't think so," Sam replied. "It's better to do it in person." All police officers hate to make these visits to inform a family that a loved one has died. The shock, the grief, the tears haunt you for days. Raw grief is hard to bear for anyone.

They exited their police car and made their way up to the front door. Sigenthaler was impressed by the pillars and front porch. A massive stain-glassed oak door greeted them. There was a brass plate next to the doorbell that read, 'Cave canem'. Sigenthaler pointed it out to Sam.

"Beware of the dog," she replied.

"How in the world . . . .," he started to say, but Sam cut him off.

"Don't ask."

They could hear the Westminster chimes going off inside the house announcing their arrival. When Dr. Lindquist answered the door, Sam introduced herself and Sigenthaler.

Sigenthaler's jaw dropped and his eyes bulged out when he saw at her. He was looking at a goddess! If Dr. Lindquist noticed his reaction, she ignored it.

Ingrid Lindquist was about five feet six inches tall. She had Scandinavian blonde hair and pale blue eyes. Her hair was very thick and soft, and seemed to float around her neck and shoulders as she turned from side to side when addressing them. She had the hourglass figure of a professional model. Sam took a sideways glance at Sigenthaler as Dr. Lindquist invited them in. "Shut your mouth," Sam whispered as they followed Dr. Lindquist into the living room. Guinevere eyed them suspiciously. The dog went immediately from one to the other, sniffing them and wagging her tail.

"Sorry about that," Dr. Lindquist said. "She is still a puppy at heart."

Sam surveyed the upscale living room and noticed the throw rug was in a Bloomsbury-esque print in pale raspberry. She saw two expensive striped chairs and candles floating in water in a dark blue bowl on an antique table. Dr. Lindquist directed them to sit on an Italian motif sofa set. She sat down opposite them and smiled.

"Would you like a cup of coffee?" she asked.

They both declined and a short silence followed. Then Dr. Lindquist spoke.

"I will take care of removing the car once my husband comes home. He will know whom to call." Sam and Sigenthaler looked at one another. Dr. Lindquist looked puzzled. "Aren't you here about my damaged car? I left it at the hospital parking lot last night after a tree fell on it." Guinevere was lying on the rug next to her, looking bored.

Sam and Sigenthaler remained silent. "Are you sure you wouldn't like a cup of coffee?" Dr. Lindquist offered again. "I just made it a few minutes ago. It's a Swedish blend and very tasty."

Sam was at a loss. In an instant she realized how bizarre this situation was. Dr. Lindquist had no clue as to their visit. Sam had no choice but to come right out with it. "We are very sorry to tell you like this, but your husband was found murdered this morning."

The atmosphere in the room suddenly changed. Dr. Lindquist didn't say a word. She just remained silent staring at Sam. She showed no expression and didn't emote any feelings. Her face turned to stone. Sam wondered if she had gone into shock. A few tense moments passed. Sigenthaler was getting antsy. Sam touched his arm.

"Sorry," Ingrid said. "Could you repeat what you just said?"

Sam lowered her voice and told her again.

Dr. Lindquist immediately got up and went to the kitchen. When she returned she had a fresh cup of coffee in her hand. She sat down again. She slowly sipped the steaming black liquid. She looked at Sam and then stared out the living room window. If she was processing the news, she did so in total silence. She wasn't with them in the room. Her thoughts had taken her to a different place.

Sam and Sigenthaler didn't say anything and just waited in silence. They could hear the ticking of a pendulum clock somewhere in the house. Guinevere stirred and looked up at her mistress and settled down again. Sam noticed Sigenthaler sat frozen. It seemed as if he was afraid to move as he stared at Dr. Lindquist. Sam didn't know what to do or say, other than just to wait out the deafening silence. She realized that this was one of those moments in life when destiny interrupts us and assaults our very being.

After what seemed like an eternity, Dr. Lindquist turned her attention to Sam. "What do we do next? I mean, where do we go from here?"

Sam told her that she would have to identify the body in the morgue located in the basement of the hospital. Dr. Lindquist nodded. She asked Sam to drive her there since she didn't have a car. Sam said she would. Dr. Lindquist locked the front door after petting Guinevere on the head and saying goodbye. She then followed Sam to the waiting squad car.

CHAPTER 5

It was eight thirty on Saturday morning, and Chief Johns sat behind his desk at the police station. He had papers and reports strewn on his desk and around the room. To the casual observer, the office looked like a chaotic mess. He seldom met with people in his office because of the clutter. In fact, his office had become an inside joke at the station. He didn't care though. He knew where every scrap of paper was and could lay his hands on it anytime he needed it.

He was looking over his notes and was clearly agitated. He had received a phone call from the chairman of the Monroe Police and Fire Commission, Roger Nussbaum, Friday afternoon. Mr. Nussbaum was also the chairman of Governor Bartholf's newly formed Crime Commission. Nussbaum was not happy. He was an arrogant, outspoken, intense and impatient man. This was the third homicide in Monroe since his appointment to the Governor's task force. He got the chairmanship, because he touted the low crime statistics in Monroe, and now he felt his reputation was on the line. His colleagues were on him about the negative press Monroe was getting. So far the governor hadn't said anything to him, but politics were politics, and these murders could not be tolerated! The pressure he felt in Madison was ramping up! He was afraid for his political future.

Johns privately thought that the crime commission was no more than a toothless political stunt by the governor. From the monthly statistics he received from Madison, the crime rate in Wisconsin remained pretty much constant; neither going up or down very much. But it was a major talking point for Nussbaum, and the constant chatter about it was slowly driving him crazy.

"A famous heart surgeon murdered!" Nussbaum screamed. "This is not acceptable! Not in Monroe!"

He told the chief to solve the murder as quickly as possible. He personally would be expecting updates on the PD's efforts to find the killer. He had to maintain his tough political stance on crime! He reminded the chief again and again that Dr. Buckle was a very high profile heart surgeon, and the news media would be all over this murder. Johns agreed with the news media piece, and that was one of his own concerns. Not only had the Madison newspapers been nagging him for comments, but Jake Nueberger from the Monroe Press was getting on his nerves. Understandably, the citizens of Monroe were on edge. All the stress and criticism surrounding the murder were causing Johns distress, and he wasn't sleeping very well at night.

Chief Johns was meeting with Sam and Sigenthaler in fifteen minutes. They were coming in to report any progress they had made in the past twenty-four hours regarding the case. He was hoping that something significant would turn up. Nussbaum had scheduled him to go to Washington, D.C. to a police conference months ago. He couldn't back out now, because he was one of the speakers. When he pleaded his case to Nussbaum, he was turned down flat. The chief wasn't only representing Monroe but the whole state of Wisconsin! So he temporarily relinquished his involvement in the case and would have to rely heavily on Detective Gates.

As Johns gathered up his notes and got ready to leave his office, the look on his wife's face at breakfast that morning flashed across his mind. He had to cancel their shopping trip to Chicago, which she had organized two weeks ago. They were to meet her sister, Mary, and her husband on Michigan Avenue for shopping and then onto Navy Pier for dinner. Johns had looked forward to the get-away trip, but a job is a job. Beth understood that he had irregular working hours, and she accepted this as part of their marriage. But the disappointment still stung. Remorse and guilt followed him as he made his way down the well-worn, green-speckled linoleum hallway to the squad room. Somehow he would have to make it up to her.

When the Chief entered the squad room, he saw Detective Gates and Captain Sigenthaler sitting at their desks waiting for him. Sam offered to get him a cup of coffee, which he gladly accepted. She quickly returned a few moments later with a steaming mug of black coffee. He took a sip and thanked her.

Then he thanked them both for coming in and apologized for screwing up their weekend. Sam sat down again, and Johns stood in front of their desks, briefing them on Nussbaum's anxious call for a quick arrest. Sigenthaler mumbled under his breath, but Johns ignored it.

Johns looked down at his notes. "Let me summarize again where we are. Then each of you can report on your progress. Okay?" They both nodded.

"As you are aware, the call came in early Friday morning that a body had been discovered in the parking lot at the Country Club. The call was made by an employee, Fritz Figi. He had reported to work early to check for any storm damage. He noticed the body lying in the parking and assumed it had been hit by lightning. After a closer look, he wasn't so sure and called the police.

"Officer Kennickson was the first to arrive, checked out the body and declared it a crime scene. He then taped off the area. Dr. Ken Anderson was called, and he confirmed that the victim was indeed dead. He said Dr. Buckle was shot three times and bled out on the pavement. He estimated the time of death was between seven and ten p.m. Thursday night. The body was bagged and taken to the morgue for an autopsy. He reported that the three bullet holes lined up with the shirt and jacket of the victim. No burn marks were found. After he removed the bullets from the victim, he determined that the gun used was a Smith and Wesson .38 Special. From the victim's wallet, we found his driver's license and ascertained that he was Dr. George Andrew Buckle who worked at the hospital. His wife, Dr. Ingrid Lindquist, later identified the body."

Johns paused and took another sip of coffee. He saw the two officers nodding in agreement. Then he continued.

"We can surmise that robbery wasn't the motive, since five twenty-dollar bills were found in his money clip. Also, the BMW parked beside his body was untouched. It looked as if Dr. Buckle was approaching his car from the direction of the bar when he was shot. No shell casings were found at the scene. Well, that's about it. Any questions?"

He looked at Sigenthaler, who was reviewing his own notes. The captain was a fifteen-year veteran of the police force and was married with teenage children. He was of average height, well-built and balding, and wore wire-framed glasses. He was a no-nonsense cop who enjoyed bowling, card playing and deer hunting. Sigenthaler looked more like a college professor than a cop.

He looked up and saw Johns staring at him. "My turn?" he asked. Johns nodded. Sigenthaler picked up his notes and glanced at them.

"After some effort we found what looked like a boot print along the hedgerow," he began. "Even though the ground was soft, due to the storm, the print wasn't very clear. We surmised that the killer came through the pedestrian entrance at the far end of the parking lot. He may have had a vehicle waiting for him on Lincoln Avenue. We think that the killer either got into a car or just walked away after the murder. We only found the one boot print, so we think the killer acted alone. Casts were made of the print, and the boot was determined to be size nine. Also, we found no identifiable tire marks on the street." He paused and looked at the chief. No questions, so he continued.

"I canvassed the houses along Lincoln Avenue, but no one saw anything. The residents were all inside their homes due to the ferocity of the storm. The bartender wasn't much help either. He said that Dr. Buckle's wife called him a few minutes before he left. He was agitated after receiving the call. He also said that Dr. Buckle was pretty lit up when he left the bar. As the doctor was walking toward his car, the bartender said he didn't see anyone else in the area. We are still interviewing people in the area of the Country Club, so far without any success." Sigenthaler paused. No one said anything.

Sam picked up her notes. "First of all, I think the murder must have been a crime of passion. I also think it was premeditated. Anyone deliberately going out into a raging storm like the one Thursday night to kill someone was as driven as the storm. The anger, or whatever it was that was in control of the killer, clearly overrode the severity of the storm. The killer must have known Dr. Buckle and his movements. How else would he know that the doctor would be there?" Sam stopped to let her commentary sink in. The chief nodded. She continued.

"The reaction from Dr. Buckle's wife when we told her about the murder was most peculiar. The total control of her emotions, not showing any reaction to the news of murder of her husband, raised some suspicions in my mind. She didn't appear to be sad, nervous or angry. She seemed detached. Maybe she was in shock, but I think it went deeper than that. We need to interview her. She probably has a lot to tell us about Buckle, and I think she may have some useful information about the murder."

Johns interrupted her. "Do you think she was somehow involved in his death?"

"I am not sure. I don't think so, but I can't rule it out."

Johns looked at Sigenthaler, who nodded.

"Do you think the murderer acted alone?" Johns asked.

"I guess our investigation will have to answer that question," Sam replied.

Johns reflected for a moment. "Don't you find it interesting that we only learn about someone's life after they are dead?" he said. "We interview their loved ones, their colleagues and friends. We probe into family secrets to get at the truth. In the process, we get half-truths and lies. It seems that everyone has something to hide. We will investigate and try to get to the truth through this maze of deception. I just want to caution you both that we don't want to get side-tracked and end up in the weeds. We need to pursue the facts wherever they take us."

Sam was staring at him during his philosophical moment. "Nice speech," she said. Johns laughed.

"Is the political pressure from Nussbaum turned up on this one?" Sigenthaler asked.

Johns laughed again, "Busted!"

"So where do we go from here?" Sam asked.

"I leave Monday morning for Washington D.C. and will be gone a week. Sam, I want you to interview Dr. Buckle's wife and get whatever information you can from her." He turned to Sigenthaler and told him to go the hospital and interview anyone who knew the doctor. "Also I want you to interview the folks on Lincoln Avenue again. Someone must have seen something. Call me in D.C. if anything turns up."

As he was leaving, Johns stopped. He suddenly remembered something. "A woman by the name of Keegan called in and said she may have seen something on the night of the murder. She lives on Lincoln Avenue."

"Lincoln Avenue?" Sigenthaler said. "I interviewed her husband, and he said they didn't see anything."

"Well, you and Sam go see her and check it out," Johns replied. With that he left them standing there, when he suddenly turned around again.

"Just one more thing before I leave," he said. "I don't have to remind you that Monroe is a treasure trove of gossip. And if I remember correctly, Jake Neuberger at the Monroe Press is a shirt-tail relation to your Sigenthaler family. Isn't that right, Detective?"

"Yeah, he's a second or third cousin on my mother's side," Sigenthaler muttered.

"We all need to be tight lipped on this case," the Chief warned. "Any questions?"

No reply came from either of them.

"All right then."

CHAPTER 6

Mrs. Lois Keegan, who lived in the house on Lincoln Avenue directly across from the pedestrian entrance to the Country Club, called the police after Alfred, her husband, told her about the visit from Sigenthaler. She wasn't home when the police came to their front door. Only later did she remember seeing something of interest during the night of storm. She was seventy-eight years old, stood five foot four, had short gray hair, and wore black rimmed bifocals. Both she and her husband retired from the Swiss Colony company thirteen years ago. She was a secretary and Alfred worked in maintenance.

Lois had written down what she thought she remembered from the stormy night. Her memory wasn't the best these days, so writing things down had become a habit for her. She had handwritten notes scattered all around the house. Alfred just ignored them.

The police had made an appointment to see her at nine on Saturday morning. After reviewing her notes on the night of the storm, she decided to leave out the part about Alfred and their little dog hiding under the bed during the storm. The dog was definitely afraid of thunder and lightning.

Lois had gotten up early. This was the first time in her life that she had any formal contact with the police, and she was nervous. After vacuuming the living room twice, she dusted everything from the front door to the kitchen. She was determined to make a good impression.

What to serve the officers once they arrived was a concern. Just to be sure, she arranged a cheese tray on her mother's antique round cut-glass plate. Then she made egg salad sandwiches and cut them into triangular shapes. She had leftover bars and cookies from a family dinner that she arranged on a plate. The last thing to do was to make a pot of fresh coffee, which was now percolating in the kitchen alongside the rest of the food.

Alfred thought all this fuss was silly, so Lois dispatched him to his utility shed in the backyard until after the police left. She told him to take Pepe to the shed as well. Pepe was a short-haired Chihuahua that their youngest son gave them to take care of three years ago when he moved to Janesville. She was convinced that the little dog had an attitude and possibly mental problems. He was very hyper and yipped constantly at any strange noises, especially the mailman. For some reason, the little fellow wanted to sleep with them at night, which drove Alfred crazy. Their son had turned a deaf ear to their pleadings to take him back.

All was ready. Lois was wearing a freshly pressed cotton dress and her hair looked nice. It was five to nine when she saw the two police cars pull up and park on the street in front of her ranch-style house. She noticed that the two officers were engaged in conversation as they approached the front door. One of the officers was a woman, and the other was a man with a slight limp. She waved at them from the living room window as they approached.

Lois opened the door and greeted the officers. She took them into the living room and was about to ask them to sit down when, to her astonishment, Pepe appeared from out of nowhere barking very loudly. He raced toward the officers and starting jumping and dancing around them in his dog-like neurotic manner. As he smelled their shoes and uniforms, Sigenthaler gave him a little shove with his foot.

Instantly the little dog went wild. He jumped on Sigenthaler's gimpy leg and madly started humping it! The atmosphere in the room turned into one of shock and disbelief. Lois screamed. She quickly backed away and stared in horror as the horny little dog was humping away.

Sigenthaler was perplexed. This attack on his leg caught him by surprise. He shouted at the dog and tried to shake him off, but the little creature seemed to be glued to his leg. Then he started moving his body to and fro trying to shake the dog off. The dog was determined! His full, round black eyes were laser-like on Sigenthaler's pant leg. Sigenthaler's face flushed with anger. His cheeks were beet-red as he gave one swift and violent kick of his bad leg. The dog went flying through the air and rolled over and over and landed up against the sofa. Lois shrieked. In an instant the dog was back again, humping like a mechanized tractor piston.

Alfred suddenly appeared from the kitchen and immediately sized up the situation. He went for Pepe and grabbed him off Sigenthaler's leg. The dog struggled and barked in protest. As they disappeared back into the kitchen and out the back door, Lois collapsed on the sofa. "I told my son that he should have had that dog fixed!"

Sigenthaler lost it! He was cursing in the most egregious way. Sam grabbed him by the arm and led him outside to the front porch. After a few moments, he calmed down. Sigenthaler looked down at his pants leg and saw the stain. "Oh God," he screamed. "I am going to kill that little shit dog!"

Sam told him again to calm down. Sigenthaler was beside himself. "I am going to burn these pants!" he shouted to no one in particular. Then without saying another word, he turned and walked to his police car. Sam noticed that his limp was more pronounced. He jumped into the squad car and sped away. Sam watched him disappear around the corner and then went back into the house. She found Lois sitting on the sofa, crying and staring into space as if in shock. Sam gently touched her arm and smiled at her.

"Don't worry," she said. "No harm was done."

Lois looked at her and asked in a low voice if the police were going to arrest her. Sam assured her that everything was okay and there would be no arrests. Lois took some comfort in this and apologized over and over again.

After she had calmed down, Lois went into the kitchen and returned with a tray of goodies for the light mid-morning lunch. Then she asked Sam if she wanted a cup of coffee, and Sam thanked her.

As they sat chewing their food, Sam needed to get her back to the reason for the visit.

"You called the police station and said you may have seen something of interest on the night of the storm," Sam began.

Lois seemed relived for the change of subject and to get her mind off that damn dog.

"Yes, I do believe I saw something," she replied. Then she excused herself and went back into the kitchen. When she returned she held a piece of paper. She quickly read it over and began to tell her story.

"On the night of that terrible storm, Pepe was so afraid and shaking that he hid under our bed. Alfred joined him there to comfort him." Lois had forgotten she wasn't going to mention that part to the police.

"There was no way I was diving under the bed, so I stood by my picture window watching the lightning show. Suddenly, I saw a strange thing, you know, something out-of-place. A man walked up the street from the south and stopped at the path that led into the County Club. He paused for about a minute and then disappeared through the hedge."

"Are you sure it was a man?" Sam asked.

"Well, I think it was. The rain was coming down really hard, but my impression was that it was a man. He was dressed up like a cowboy."

"A cowboy?"

"Yes. He had on a cowboy hat pulled low over his face, and he was wearing a rain slicker or duster or whatever you call it. You know, like the cowboys wear on television westerns. He held on to his hat as the wind and rain pounded him."

"Did you see him again?"

"No. Shortly after that I went into the bedroom to check on Pepe and Alfred. Is what I saw important? The whole neighborhood is talking about the murder."

Sam wrote down Lois's account in her notebook.

"About what time did you see him?"

"I don't know exactly, somewhere between seven thirty and eight, I think."

"Is there anything else you remember?"

"No, I don't think so."

Sam thanked her. The interview was over. Sam was satisfied that she had gotten all the information that Lois had. They made small talk, and then Sam announced that she had to leave. She thanked her for the goodies and coffee and told her not to worry about the dog incident, as she was sure that Sigenthaler would get over it.

At the front door, Lois asked her how Jerome was doing. She could tell by the puzzled look on Sam's face that she didn't know who she was talking about.

"Jerome Pagel is my sister's grandson. He is a student at the UW in Madison and is doing a summer intern at the police department."

Sam thought for a minute, and then it clicked. The chief had requested a summer intern to organize and file police records, clear out some of the paper chaos at the station and tidy up the evidence room. She had seen him at the station but didn't know his name.

"Jerome is doing fine. We all like him." Then Sam left Lois standing at the front door and headed for her squad car. She needed to report this mysterious man dressed as a cowboy to Sigenthaler.

CHAPTER 7

Saturday morning found Father Bernard seated comfortably in his favorite overstuffed chair in the rectory. The sun was brightly shining in through the east window of living room. Father Bernard was the Catholic priest at St. Michael's Church on 14th Street in Monroe. His nest of white hair and vibrant blue eyes made him look older than his forty-three years. He had just returned from a two-day conference in Lake Geneva late the night before and was now trying to catch up on the happenings in the city. He held a copy of the Monroe Press in his hand. The news of the Dr. Buckle murder had made its way to the conference, so he was anxious to get back to Monroe. He was sure that he would get the latest gossip on the case from one or more of his many parishioners.

Father Bernard was the eldest of five boys in his family. He was born and raised in Watertown, Wisconsin. His father was a machinist at a local factory. His mom was from Juda, Wisconsin, and a stay-at-home mother. His grandparents, Joyce and Wendell Wenger, owned a dairy farm in Jefferson Township about four miles east of Monroe on Middle Juda Road.

His fondest childhood memories were the many summers he spent on the farm helping with chores and enjoying the relaxed pace of life. He loved his grandparents and was always eager to help around the farm. Even cleaning out the dairy barn alongside his grandfather was a joy for him. He learned the names of all the cows, and they seemed more like people to him than Holsteins. He would also spend hours watching the sheep and chickens. The animals fascinated him.

His grandmother made him feel special when she baked chocolate chip cookies with nuts in them just for him. Grandpa thought those cookies were pretty special too! The noon meal was exceptional. The hired man, Glen Broge, would join them, and they all were very relaxed as they sat around the dinner table. Fresh cut flowers in the center of the oak table came from Grandma's cutting garden. His grandmother always said grace before every meal. Mr. Broge was a very nice man and would ask Bernard non-intrusive questions to keep the conversation lively. Bernard was the center of attention, and he loved it! After dinner he would sneak into his grandfather's bedroom and watch him taking a thirty-minute nap before going back to work. The gently rhythm of his snoring was fun to watch. For Bernard, being on the farm was the idyllic life.

The Jaeggi farm was just to the east of his grandparents, and he spent many hours there visiting and playing with their kids. Going into Monroe on Friday nights was a special treat. Not only did he get to ride in the back of Grandpa's old farm pickup truck with his friends, he was given fifty cents to spend on whatever he desired.

Bernard always started his night at Ruf's Confectionary, located on the southwest corner of the square, where he bought a bag of popcorn. The store was his favorite. It had a big ceiling fan running overhead that chased away the flies in the summer. The screen door with a tight spring was hard for him to open, but it didn't seem to dissuade the flies. The domed glass counters featured lots of different kinds of candy and chocolates. It would take him forever to make up his mind what to buy, while his grandparents giggled in delight.

Ruf's was a favorite shop for the locals. They could get a fountain coke, an ice cream cone, a newspaper or a magazine, and weigh themselves for free on a huge scale sitting next to the front door. It was one of those anchor shops on the square that seemed to bind people together in the heart of Monroe.

Walking around the square at night seemed to have the same magic as being at a carnival. Bernard was frequently wedged in with all the other local folks who shopped and walked and visited each other. While his grandparents did their banking and shopping, he would let the crowd push him along as he looped the square several times with the Jaeggi kids. In the center of it all stood the Romanesque-style court house that was all lit up like a castle in a fairy tale. The bells in the clock tower would ring out regularly announcing the time.

On Sunday mornings, going to church at St. Michael's was a given. No excuses for missing Mass! He would parade in with his grandparents and a couple of the Jaeggi kids. He felt very welcomed, and the people were always nice and friendly. After all, he was Wendell Wenger's grandson, and everyone knew Wendell.

Bernard's mother, a devote Catholic, prayed to God every night that her eldest son would become a priest. As an adolescent, he had many doubts about her expectations. He just couldn't see himself dressed in black robes.

She would tell him that God was calling him into the priesthood, but he wasn't listening. As he grew older, he realized that she was wearing him down. During Mass, he started to imagine himself as a priest.

When Bernard turned eighteen, Father Thomas from St. Henry's in Watertown, (who Bernard suspected of being in collaboration with his mother), singled him out several times and spoke in glowing language about the virtues of joining the priesthood. He told him about the ancient calling of priests 2,000 years ago and the sacrifices they made. The fact that God only calls special saints to become priests wasn't lost on Bernard.

To please them both, and to satisfy his own curiosity, he applied and was accepted to seminary at Mt. Olive in Milwaukee after high school graduation. He told himself that he wasn't really signing up for the priesthood, only to discern whether or not he felt truly called to be a priest.

After a regime of daily prayers, daily Mass, frequent confession and spiritual readings he started to feel the call. This reflective time awakened deep religious feelings within him that just seemed right. The feelings reminded him of the times he spent on his grandparents' farm when he felt close to God. He began to think that his true vocation in life was to be an ordained priest. But he still wasn't sure. Maybe reading the Bible again and asking God to guide him in his decision would be the answer. So he started with Genesis to begin his journey. He focused on the task at hand in the solitude his room every night. Sometimes he stayed up until one or two in the morning.

Bernard was getting discouraged. Nothing leapt off the sacred pages until one late night when he was slowly working his way through the book of Ezekiel. Chapter twenty-two verse thirty stopped him cold. "I looked for a man among them who would build up a wall and stand before me in the gap on behalf of the land so I would not have to destroy it, but I found none." The visual imagery of the passage stunned him. The 'aha' moment was accompanied by astounding clarity. Bernard immediately dropped to his knees and thanked God. He wanted to be that man in the gap!

His path was clear! He felt that God had revealed himself to him in the quiet solitude of the night. He spent the next five years in seminary and was ordained a priest with the vows of obedience and celibacy ingrained in his soul.

He heard in seminary that priests choose the calling of their own free will, but he wondered if his mother hadn't given him more than a little shove. His mother told him once that priests can, "make jam from the fallen fruit of the Garden of Eden." Maybe his mother should have been a priest!

After a career of serving several parishes in Minnesota and northern Wisconsin, Father Bernard was finally was able to move to Monroe four years ago to serve St. Michael's. His life's experiences as a priest taught him that it is not just a job; it becomes your personal identity. Coming to Monroe was coming home for him. Being a priest at St. Michael's was a dream come true.

When asked why he loved the city of Monroe and Green County so much, he would always say, "It is very green in the summer and very white in the winter. It has a very good church and a very good priest and a very good pub!" His parishioners loved him.

As he sat reading the article by Jake Neuberger, a former altar boy at St. Michael's, he felt sad. The violence surrounding the murder and the victim concerned him. He shook his head at the thought of it. A renowned heart surgeon, who did so much good in his life, had had his life tragically taken away. Who in Monroe would do such a horrible thing? He said a silent prayer for the family.

After he finished the article, he made his way to the kitchen and poured himself a cup of coffee. He had left a packet of materials from the conference on the kitchen table from the night before. He returned to his chair with the coffee in one hand and the packet in the other. Once he was settled in again, he opened the packet and reviewed the conference agenda and notes. He would need to report his findings to the Parish Council.

The theme of the conference was the future of the church. He wasn't very thrilled about the topic, because it always brought out the glass-is-half-empty crowd. It was a mystery to him why men of faith seemed at times to have so little faith.

The first topic discussed concerned the slight drop in active dioceses, parishes and priests in Wisconsin. One priest spoke about the tragedy and sadness of starting to think about closing parishes. Actually, he could think of only one in a remote area of northern Wisconsin. The priest spoke passionately about the emotional trauma for the parishioners who were losing the very church where their children were baptized and where their parents were buried. The passion in his plea was like describing a funeral Mass for a deceased church. His oratory was received in silence.

What to do about the future shortage of priests was another topic. The smaller parishes had only one priest, and the speaker was covering two or three other parishes like a circuit rider. Father Bernard was thankful for the large congregation at St. Michael's and lifted up a short silent prayer.

Also, the number of lapsed Catholics not attending Mass was a disturbing trend. On this point there was general agreement. How did the drop-outs view their faith since they rarely came to church? One priest stood up and sarcastically compared parishes to convenience stores saying, "People now-a-days come to church only for the Eucharist, baptisms, marriages and funerals!" He got a laugh at his comments, but all the priests seemed to concur.

Another galling subject was that the priests were encouraged to get more involved with the financial affairs of their parishes. When this concern was lifted up, audible groans were heard throughout the assemblage. The priests felt that they were already stretched by their workloads and had precious little time for anything else. Besides, they were trained to bless, not to budget! Once again, Father Bernard felt blessed that his parish in Monroe was doing okay financially.

The last discussion point lifted up was the sacrament of confession or reconciliation. Statistical findings were presented that showed an alarming decline in Catholics going to confession. They were ignoring a fundamental rite meant to keep them holy and close to God. The report also stated that while entire congregations receive communion, the confessionals remain almost empty. This revelation came as no surprise to Father Bernard.

The reasons given for the decline were troublesome. The Bishop speaking about this point summarized it as a 'cultural war' between society and the church. He theorized that we are living in a culture that tells us that we aren't responsible for our actions when we sin. He blamed Hollywood and the news media for the changing attitudes toward God and religion. "And where are the parents?" he asked. He felt that the decline in moral values started in the home. The lack of religious education was missing in early childhood, and that was alarming. "Were moral issues no longer important to the parents?" he queried. He finished his presentation and shared some personal interviews that he had with older people in various congregations. He said that they were all perplexed about the lower attendance at mass and they were asking, "What's happening in the church today, and what is its future?"

As Father Bernard sat his cozy chair pondering these church issues, an image suddenly flashed across his mind. It was a remembrance.

About a week ago, he had happened upon a middle-aged woman on her knees praying in one of the middle pews. He immediately recognized her. The hour was late, after seven at night, and he was surprised to see her there. He stayed very still and silent as he watched. The fading sunlight came in through the stain glass windows.

Her name was Diane Fouts. She had two children and was married to a local lawyer. She was of average height and had short cropped auburn hair. In addition to her volunteer work at the church, she was employed full-time at the hospital. They were all alone in the dimly lit church. He stood and watched her in silence.

While waiting in the rear of the church, he looked around the sanctuary. A stained glass window to his right depicted St. Michael with a spear in his hand posed to strike Satan and to hurl him for all eternity into the burning pool of hell. Written on the shield strapped to his arm was the Latin phase, "Quis ut Deus," "Who is like God." Whenever Father Bernard looked at the stained glass depiction of the archangel, he was always reminded that St. Michael is the Guardian of the Church.

He could clearly see Christ on the Crucifix behind the altar. To the left were the pulpit and a statue of Mary. On the right was the lectern where the Scriptures were read.

Suddenly the woman stood up and genuflected. Then she made her way to the rear of the church and noticed the priest standing there. She had smiled at him. "Hi, Father," she said in a low soft voice.

Father Bernard greeted her and asked her if she was okay. She told him that she was having personal problems and needed to talk to God. He could make out a bruise mark on her neck. He could also tell from her demeanor that something was definitely wrong.

He had asked if going to confession would help. She thanked him and declined his offer. She said that something terrible had happened to her and only another woman would truly understand her plight. Seeing the surprised look on his face, she quickly apologized. He started to say something but changed his mind. She thanked him again, crossed herself with Holy Water and left him standing there all alone. The implication of her response was only too clear to him, a criticism that he had heard many times before.

How can an unmarried priest relate to a married woman having marital problems?

Bernard now eased himself out of his soft chair and walked to the window on the north side of his living room. It faced the street. He held the newspaper in his left hand. As he watched the traffic pass by, his mind drifted back to the problem of confession. He agreed that fewer parishioners were coming in for confession, but he maintained his own scheduled times and dates for the faithful.

Then abruptly, his thoughts sprang back to the troubled woman. He seldom saw her husband, Jeff Fouts, in church. Fouts was only a Christmas and Easter Catholic. The priest never saw him in church other than those two services. Diane and the kids attended regularly.

So what was is it that she can't confide in a priest? Did it have anything to do with the bruise on her neck? He had heard the rumors that her marriage was in turmoil. Perhaps that is why she couldn't confide in her husband either. She worked as an out-patient counselor at the Monroe Regional Medical Center. Maybe something happened there?

Something about the woman was nagging at him. He couldn't put his finger on it. Maybe he could talk to her again, and the next time she would be more open to talk about her feelings.

He refilled his coffee cup and went back into the living room and re-read the article on Dr. Buckle's murder.

CHAPTER 8

I was Monday afternoon, and the sun had broken through the clouds and was shining into the living room of Dr. Ingrid Lindquist. She was sitting on her living room sofa with her dog Guinevere at her feet. She was wearing light khaki pants and a pink silk blouse.

Sitting across from her in an overstuffed flowered armchair was her sister-in-law, Elisabeth Anne Stuart. Stuart had just flown in from London after Lindquist called her about Dr. Buckle's death. Getting a last minute transatlantic flight was expensive, but Elisabeth felt she needed to give emotional support to Ingrid.

They were drinking Manhattans made with Canadian whisky. On the coffee table in front of them sat a serving tray with assorted cheeses and crackers. The Green County cheeses were Ingrid's favorites: Colby Jack, aged Swiss and a mild Cheddar. Elisabeth commented that the cheeses had better flavor and texture than European cheeses. Ingrid agreed. Since moving to Monroe, the one thing that had been a pleasant surprise was the superb five-star rating for local cheeses. Whether used in cooking or arranged on a serving tray for guests, the cheeses were the best in the world!

Elisabeth was dressed in a tailored beige suit accented by a colorful maroon neck scarf. An expensive silver oak leaf brooch was pinned to her jacket. She was tall, like her brother, fair-skinned and buxom. She had a sophisticated aura about her that was blithe and debonair. As they casually chatted the afternoon away, they were waiting for Detective Gates who had called earlier that morning and scheduled an interview for four o'clock.

Elisabeth had flown from Heathrow to Chicago to Madison, where Ingrid had picked her up. They drove directly to the Medical Center morgue so she could view the body. After the autopsy on Friday, Dr. Ken had held the body at the request of Dr. Lindquist, so that Dr. Buckle's sister could see it before he was sent to the Kraemer Funeral Home for cremation.

Elisabeth was going to take the black urn back to Birmingham, England, to have it buried in the family plot alongside her parents. Since she came from a very small family with no living relatives, she planned to have a short graveside service with only her husband and the local vicar attending. Ingrid told her that she wouldn't be going back with her to England, and Elisabeth agreed with her decision. What would be the point, Ingrid mused.

Guinevere suddenly jumped up and raced to the front door as the Westminster chimes rang out. Ingrid Lindquist got up and casually walked to the front door to welcome Detective Gates. She told Guinevere to go lie down after the dog sniffed Sam's shoes and then invited the detective into the living room. In the hallway, Sam noticed a framed Italian print hanging on the wall by Pietro Pezzati, "A Woman Forsaken." She didn't remember seeing it on her previous visit.

Ingrid introduced Sam to Elisabeth, who remained seated and nodded to her. Ingrid motioned for Sam to sit down in a comfortable chair next to Stuart. She offered her a Manhattan, but Sam turned it down, opting for a cup of coffee instead. Elisabeth passed her the cheese tray as Ingrid went to the kitchen and returned with the coffee in a flowered porcelain cup. As Sam sipped her coffee, she admired a strawberry field crewelwork fabric draped over the sofa. Somehow, she must have missed the subtle elegance of the house on her first visit. The entire house seemed to be awash with a very expensive décor. Guinevere let out a low moan and stretched herself out on the warm carpet beside Lindquist and closed her eyes.

"Thank you for seeing me," Sam began. "I am very sorry for your loss." She looked at both women. Ingrid asked if it was okay for Elisabeth to stay during the questioning, which was okay with Sam. Then they just stared at her with no expression. However, they were giving her their full attention. Sam felt as if she was about to give them the weather report. The atmosphere in the room was cold. She pulled out her spiral-bound blue notebook and a pen. She was ready to start her inquiry.

"Police Chief Johns has put Captain Sigenthaler and myself in charge of the case. If you have any questions or comments, please feel free to interrupt me as I ask you some routine questions, okay?" The women smiled at her and continued to sip their drinks.

"At this stage of the investigation, we think that the murderer acted alone. We found some forensic evidence at the crime scene to suggest that. Also, we have ruled out that this was a random act of violence. The perpetrator must have known the doctor. To ignore the raging storm and wait from him to come out of the bar area of the Country Club was an act of premeditation. We think he intended to kill or harm the doctor."

Sam paused a moment to let her comments sink in. No response.

"We are probably looking for a male about five-feet, ten-inches tall. There is one possible witness, and we are not disclosing at this time what she said as we pursue our inquiries. Captain Sigenthaler is interviewing hospital staff for any information that could help us." Sam paused. The women remained quiet.

Sam looked at Dr. Lindquist and asked, "Do you know of any person or persons that may have a grudge or grievance against your husband?"

Ingrid shrugged her shoulders.

"How was he before Thursday night? Was he nervous, anxious, afraid, or was anything bothering him that you were aware of?"

Ingrid picked up her drink and took another sip and sat back comfortably on the sofa.

"I guess I may as well tell you about my honorable husband," Ingrid said in a sarcastic monotone voice. "You will probably find out anyway. My husband was a bastard. A real shit from the first water! The only reason he took this job in Monroe was to avoid any scandal on his brilliant medical record from Boston General. He left under a dark cloud, you see."

Ingrid paused and looked over to Elisabeth, who looked back and nodded her head approvingly.

"His plan was to spend some time here in Monroe, and then move on to the Mayo Clinic in Rochester, Minnesota. He felt that at the clinic in Rochester he could re-start his career and re-establish his reputation as a heart surgeon to achieve some exposure on the international stage. But like all brilliant men, he had some serious flaws. He could be absolutely charming on the one hand and nasty, brutish and amoral on the other. He had a serious drinking problem. He said that it was brought on by the stress of playing God during his many surgeries. Also, in his self-centered egotistical mind, he thought that having sex with other women was therapeutic and relaxed him and kept him sane. But of course, this womanizing came at a cost." Ingrid stopped talking and briefly looked out the window. No one said anything.

"You asked me if my husband had any enemies. If I were you, I would start with his many sexual conquests. He was fully aware that a ready pool of nurses at the hospital had little recourse against him if he could get them into one-on-one situations. He was constantly trolling for women or young nurses having relationship problems with either husbands or boyfriends. He seemed to have a sixth sense about it." She stopped for a moment.

Sam was taking it all in. This was not the direction that she thought her questioning would take her. Obviously, there was no love lost between Dr. Lindquist and her husband. The anger she was expressing was interesting. Maybe she just needed to get it out. Then Ingrid put her drink down. She clasped her hands very tightly revealing white knuckles. Sam took a mental note of this. The pent up frustration in this woman was very apparent.

"You are psychiatrist at the medical center, are you not?" Sam asked.

"Yes I am."

"In your opinion, what kind of person do you think would resort to murder?"

The question seemed to surprise Dr. Lindquist. "What do you mean?" she asked.

"Well, when we profile a murderer, we try to establish a motive. Obviously, robbery wasn't a motive, since your husband had one hundred dollars in his money clip when we found him."

"Okay, I see what you are driving at. Well, maybe it was revenge."

"Can you think of anything that may have happened during the past month that your husband shared with you that seemed odd?" Sam asked.

Ingrid reached up and tugged at her right ear.

"Now that you mention it, about three weeks ago he said that he was approached by a man who was obviously intoxicated in the parking lot at the hospital. The man was waiting for him, standing by George's BMW after his shift ended. He asked the man what he wanted, and he started ranting and speaking gibberish about his girlfriend, some woman named Rita.

"George said that he noticed what he thought was a gun in the man's waistband, but the strange acting man never went for it. George told the man that he had no idea who this Rita was and for him to leave immediately or he was going to call the police. Then the man mumbled something under his breath and left."

"Did he report the incident to security or the police?" Sam asked.

"I don't know. If he did, he didn't mention it to me."

I will have to check into this, Sam thought. "Do you know why your husband was at the Country Club Thursday night?"

"On Thursday nights the chef features his culinary special for the week. He usually prepares prime rib. It was George's favorite. He always insisted that I join him and his other cronies for this feast. After all the happy hour drinking, I don't know how any of them could enjoy the meal. Well anyway, it was a standing date, and I always had to clear my calendar for his Lordship. If he would have listened to the radio and paid attention to the announcements, he would have heard that the dinner was cancelled due to the threat of the severe storm warnings."

"So when you called the Country Club to talk to your husband, you knew that he would be there?"

"Of course, do you think that anything like a severe storm could get in the way of his self-centered arrogant ego and drinking?"

Sam didn't respond to the question. "Anything else come to mind?" she asked.

"Not at the moment," Ingrid said and then stood up and excused herself. "I'll be back shortly," she said and headed toward the hallway. Guinevere jumped up and followed her out of the room.

Sam turned to Elisabeth Stuart, who had been sitting very quietly. "It must have come as quite a shock to you when Dr. Lindquist phoned about your brother's murder."

"Not really," she responded in a rather bored tone of voice. "If you like, I can give you some background on the good doctor."

"Yes, that would be nice," Sam said.

"Well, he is, or was, two years younger than me. We were both raised in Birmingham, England, by middle class working parents. My dad was a business merchant, and my mum was a school teacher. The good doctor was a troubled child from the very beginning of his life. He always craved attention and did horrific things to get it. In my opinion, my parents doted on him too much and spoiled him. But he remained a hard case. You see, he was blessed with an exceptional mind. Some even called him brilliant. As he advanced with his studies, he met some very sophisticated academic scholars who encouraged him. The more he met and discussed his ideas with them, the more he resented me and my parents. He would openly criticize my parents for their lot in life. It was heartbreaking for them, since they both loved him very much. For me, I grew to hate him." Elisabeth paused and took another sip of her drink. She shifted in her chair and crossed her legs to be more comfortable.

"My mum developed breast cancer several years ago, and died nine months after the diagnosis was confirmed. Dr. Buckle couldn't find the time to see her and only came to the funeral. It all seemed like a big inconvenience for him. His attitude and behavior greatly distressed my father.

"Then a year later, Father had a stroke. Once again Dr. Buckle refused to make the trip to England to be with him. My father died without any good-byes from his son. I think he died partly from a broken heart. Well anyway, when the will was read, our parents left one-half of their meager estate to me and the other half to Dr. Buckle."

She paused and took another sip from her drink. Sam thought it odd that she always referred to her brother as Dr. Buckle and not by his first name.

Elisabeth picked up her story again. "Dr. Buckle was very upset with the will and demanded that he get three-quarters of the estate, not half. Thank God I was married to a solicitor who threatened to have him certified and committed if he persisted in his irrational views. Dr. Buckle backed down and hasn't spoken a word to me since. We didn't have much of a relationship, but his Machiavellian attitude about me and my parents was unforgivable. The only reason that his ashes are being buried next to my parents is out of my love and respect for them. They never gave up on him and loved him to the very end of their sad lives. As for me, I wouldn't have any remorse dumping his ashes in a remote pond somewhere or burying them with the ranks of the other sleepers in a Potters Field!"

Elisabeth let out a small sigh and looked at Sam with a steady gaze. Sam wasn't sure what to make of this revelation about Dr. Buckle. So he wasn't a nice guy. But what did he do to get himself murdered?

Ingrid returned to the living room with Guinevere following her. She sat down again on the sofa and looked at Elisabeth. "I was telling the detective how much I admired and loved my brother," she said. Ingrid laughed.

"Is there anything else that you can remember about your husband other than the parking lot incident that may help us?" Sam asked.

"No, that's about it. Sorry."

"I will give you my business card with my phone number on it then," Sam said and handed her the card. "If you think of anything else, please call." She then turned to Elisabeth and told her that she would also be informed about any developments in the case.

Elisabeth Stuart sat up straight and stared at Sam. "That will not be necessary, Detective. First, it is well known that only about fifty percent of murders are solved in the U.S. Secondly, if you catch the murderer, you will probably find that he had plenty of justification for his action. Thirdly, I really could not care less if you catch him or not. After the way he treated me, my parents and poor Ingrid, he got what he deserved!" For all the control in her voice, the woman's face was flushed bright red when she finished speaking.

"Well, I guess I have all the information I need for now," Sam said. She thanked them for their time and stood up.

Both women showed her to the front door and bid her good-bye. As Sam made her way down the sidewalk, she couldn't help but feel sadness for the family. She needed to meet with Sigenthaler, but first she needed to check on her mom at the nursing home.

CHAPTER 9

Sam slowly drove her car over the speed bumps into the parking lot of the Parkview Nursing Home on the north side of Monroe. Even though the hour was late, the parking lot was full of cars. After her meeting with Dr. Lindquist and her sister-in-law, Sam had tried to call Sigenthaler, but she couldn't reach him. Tomorrow is another day, she mused.

As she was walking to the visitor entrance, she met Mary Tollakson coming out. The walkway was lined with a bed of brightly colored pansies and petunias. A few red rose bushes at each end gave the beds balance and height. Mary Tollakson was the organist at the First Christian Church and volunteered her time at the nursing home. They exchanged smiles and greetings. Mary commented on how well her mother, Sharon Gates, was adjusting to her new home.

When Sam moved her mom into the nursing home for around-the-clock care, Sharon was depressed and very bitter. Prior to the move, she had had a small stroke that added to her misery. One of her first visitors at the nursing home was Mary Tollakson. After meeting with Sharon in her room and welcoming her to Monroe, Mary had offered up a short prayer. Sharon exploded with a torrent of anger and foul language. The outburst created quite a scene.

Undaunted, Mary continued seeing her. The staff workers fully understood her situation and treated Sharon with respect and dignity. Their continued friendliness and warmth worked miracles. Sharon's attitude began to soften. She started to enjoy the uniformed staff and some of the other residents there. The game changer for her was when she came to realize and appreciate what a pleasure it was to have other people around that truly cared for her. The isolation of living alone for all those years after Earl's death in Silver Bay had made her very lonely and depressed. That had been a mistake. She had to admit that Sam was right. Sharon needed other people around her to share her life. She even apologized to Mary Tollakson, whom she now considered her best friend.

Making her way down the hallway on the shiny, highly polished, linoleum floors, Sam picked up the distinct smell of pine-scented disinfectant. She passed a small alcove and saw an oversized glassed bird cage that held ten very colorful parakeets. Two residents in wheel chairs sat silently watching them. A couple of nursing home aids passed her in the hallway and nodded a silent greeting to her.

As she entered Sharon's room, she stopped when she saw Pastor Carl Peterson sitting in a green vinyl chair close to Sharon's bed, talking to her. Pastor Carl was the minister at the First Christian Church of Monroe. Her mother looked so small lying in the bed. Her graying hair and wrinkled face made her look much older than sixty-two. The difficult and traumatic life that she suffered after Earl's death had taken its toll on her.

Sharon shared her room with another woman, Hulda Anderson, who was sleeping in her single bed. Miss Anderson had thinning gray hair and a pointed nose, and made a slight snoring sound that escaped through a wide open mouth. A painted porcelain plate on the stand beside her bed featured a farm scene complete with a red barn and Holstein cows. The plate was propped up next to a dated and hand-tinted wedding photo. The groom looked stiff and uncomfortable in his tightly fitting suit. He stood beside the bride with his hand on her shoulder. The bride was sitting in a chair and smiling in her white wedding gown. Sam guessed that the photo was from the late 1800's.

Sam waited silently a few moments until Sharon saw her. She motioned her daughter to join them. Sam looked at the picture of Earl on the stand beside the bed with an assortment of various medicine bottles. Pastor Carl stood up, but Sam told him to sit back down. She would stand. They chatted briefly about the weather and Sharon's health which seemed to be fairly good.

Sam felt content being with her mother. A mother and daughter bond had developed after moving to Monroe. They could talk and laugh again. It was like a second chance for the both of them. They could even talk about Earl and remember all the good times they had before his tragic death.

Sharon suddenly announced that she was tired and needed a nap. They bid her good-bye and left after a short prayer by Pastor Carl. Sam asked Pastor Carl if he had time for a cup of coffee in the visitors lounge. He accepted.

The visitor's lounge was located near the front entrance and featured eight small tables and a coffee vending machine. The walls were painted a light cream color and hanging on them were agricultural pictures of hay and corn fields, barns, cows, and deer standing near the woods. Looking out the west window with the curtains drawn back one could see a bird feeder. It was a pleasant room with soft lighting.

The only complaint about the lounge from the visitor's point of view was the coffee. It was terrible. Sam and Pastor Carl were alone in the lounge as they sipped the horrid black liquid. They sat at one of the small tables next to the east wall.

Sam asked him for an appointment to talk about three deaths that haunted her. The deaths were the murder of her dad, Earl; the death of Brian White, a police officer who committed suicide at the Silver Bay PD; and another. Pastor Carl agreed and said he would be happy to meet with her to talk about her concerns. Sam said she would call him for an appointment.

Their conversation came to an abrupt end when a nurse in a white uniform and a nursing aid in a flower covered smock joined them in the lounge. They sat down at a table on the opposite side of the lounge next to the window. Pastor Carl stood up, bid farewell to Sam and left. As Sam was getting up to leave, the short rotund uniformed nurse asked the aid if she had heard the latest on Dr. Buckle's murder. Sam immediately sat down again and took another sip of the disgusting cold coffee. They ignored her as they lowered their voices.

The uniformed nurse, Melanie Kauer, spoke first. "I have just come from the hospital and all the talk is about the murder of Dr. Buckle. Did you know him?"

"Only to see him occasionally in the hallway on the second floor," replied the aid, Laura Schultz.

"You can't breathe a word of what I am going to tell you. It's all hush-hush at the hospital. Captain Sigenthaler from the Monroe PD is interviewing anyone who may have known Dr. Buckle or knows anything about him. Do you remember when I told you about the assault on Rita Steffes? I found out today that it was a doctor who forced himself on her. And guess who? Dr. Buckle!"

Laura gasped.

"What do you think of that?" Melanie continued. "A famous heart surgeon assaults Rita and then gets himself killed!"

"Wow," Laura said rather loudly and glanced over at Sam who seemed to be ignoring them.

"How do you know that?" she asked in a quieter voice.

"Look, nurses aren't stupid. We talk about the doctors all the time. Well, anyway, Rita told her cousin, who told Jody Schliem, who told me. I couldn't believe it. As you know, Rita has a reputation with the guys, so this news didn't come to me as any big surprise. As the story goes, she flirted with Dr. Buckle like she does with all the other docs, and one day he got her alone in the linen closet and forced himself on her."

"What did Rita do?" asked Laura, with her mouth and eyes wide open. She was squirming around in her chair and couldn't sit still.

"At first she didn't do anything. And you know why? After he was done with her, he apologized and gave her one hundred dollars in cash and left. Can you believe that?"

"One hundred dollars?" Laura mouthed.

"Yes, all in twenties."

"Then what?" asked Laura, who couldn't contain herself.

"Well, it seems that Rita tried to put some more moves on the doctor again, but he ignored her. In fact, according to Jody, he treated her rather rudely. Rita was pissed. Get this, she did it with a world renowned heart surgeon in a linen closet, and then he dismissed her like she didn't even exist."

"What did she do?"

"She made up some cock 'n bull story and told her boyfriend. You know, what's his name?"

"Dwayne Burkhalter," Laura quickly answered.

"Oh, yea, that's his name. Well, anyway, good old Dwayne gets a snoot full at the Brass Tap and tells everyone at the bar that he going to see Dr. Buckle to defend Rita's honor. What a joke! Rita told her girlfriends that Dwayne confronted the doctor in the parking lot at the hospital, and Dr. Buckle scared him off. Some kind of hero he is!"

Nurse Kauer paused and took a deep breath. She leaned back in her chair and seemed to relax. All this excitement had worn her out. Laura watched her for a while and waited and waited. She wanted more. The suspense was killing her. Then the nurse started speaking again.

"According to Rita, Dwayne is really scared. He thinks that the police may come looking for him. Frankly, I don't know what Rita sees in him. He has a bad temper, and he is the jealous type."

"Anything else?" Laura asked.

"That's all I know, except that the nurses think that Dr. Buckle was a jerk. He wasn't like the other docs. They are all pretty nice and friendly and seem to respect the people they work with. But Dr. Buckle had an attitude of being disrespectful and making people wait. He was never on time for appointments. One of the nurses who worked with him in surgery said he dripped in 'surgical arrogance'!"

"What does that mean?"

"It means that he thinks he is God!"

The two women sat in silence for a while. Then Laura said that she needed to get back to work. As she was getting up to leave, Nurse Kauer spoke again.

"Just one more thing," she said. "There is a rumor going around that there was another woman assaulted by Dr. Buckle, but no one seems to know who she is."

"Well, keep me posted," Laura said and hurriedly left the room. Then Nurse Kauer got up and followed Laura out of the room, leaving Sam sitting all alone next to the wall staring at her coffee.

CHAPTER 10

Father Bernard left the church by a side door and stood on the sidewalk. He felt exhausted. It was eleven in the morning, and he needed to take a break. He also needed a jolt of caffeine and a Danish pastry at the Coffee Bean Café on the square. Since the church was only six blocks from the downtown square, he decided to walk. The sun was shining brightly, and the birds were singing to accompany him. He was looking forward to the walk up 20th Avenue and then west onto 10th Street. In particular, he noticed the bird song of a wren. It always amazed him how such a loud song could come from such a tiny bird. It was truly one of God's miracles. As he walked along enjoying the day, he used the time to gather his thoughts.

He had been in a meeting all morning. Over his objections, the Parish Council decided to meet today. They usually scheduled their meetings at night, but due to numerous vacations and other scheduling conflicts, the majority of the council voted to gather this morning.

The council always convened in the church library. It was a large room that had a fifteen-foot oak table in the center and a well-worn, faded blue carpet. The table was surrounded by high-backed chairs and could seat as many as sixteen people when needed. The table was bequeathed to the church by a Monroe bank executive upon his death.

The library itself was surrounded by seven-foot cherry wood book cases and a high, stained glass window on the north side. The book cases were stuffed with books and overflowing. Most of the books came as donations from well-meaning congregants. As the books continued to pour in from estate sales, it was no simple task sorting out which books stayed and which books went. A small round table with a white linen table cloth was set up at the entrance to the library. On the table was a carafe of coffee, porcelain cups, freshly baked homemade cookies and cream-filled puffs from the Swiss Bakery.

Father Bernard had opened the meeting with prayer.

Kevin Larson from Adult Formation spoke on the topic of morality. This was a diversion from his usual talk on what groups were available to help men and women in their faith journeys. During his brief comments, he referenced Romans 2:7-9, "To those who by persistence in doing good seek glory, honor and immortality, he will give eternal life. But for those who are self-seeking and who reject the truth and follow evil, there will be wrath and anger. There will be trouble and distress for every human being who does evil: first for the Jew, then for the Gentile."

Father Bernard had the odd feeling that Kevin was also referencing someone on the council with his remarks. Was there a scandal? But all the members looked bored during his presentation. No one really made eye contact with him.

After he was finished, the minutes from the last meeting were read and approved.

The Finance Committee reported that the auditors for the Archdiocese were doing assessments on all the parishes. The report the committee received last week commended St. Michael's on the completed assessment and gave a glowing endorsement to the parish. No comments were given or questions asked after the report.

Donald Ganshert was a fussbudget, and he was constantly worrying about church finances. For some reason that he couldn't fully explain, he was afraid that the church would run out of money. He was a depression-era adolescent who had lived through the trauma that accompanied the possible loss of the homesteaded family farm. The other council members recognized his ongoing anxiety for what it was and made allowances.

Last month Ganshert had made the suggestion to put the weekly contributions into the bulletin. He felt that people needed to be reminded weekly to give generously to the church. So, he picked today to argue his case, which took thirty minutes. Everyone weighed in on the pros and cons of his idea. After all the discussion, no action was taken. The subject was then put on the agenda for the next meeting.

Father Bernard was not happy. Why don't they simply agree to put the damn thing in the bulletin! He felt a headache coming on and wanted this meeting to end. He got up from his chair, walked over to the white table and picked out two chocolate chip cookies from the serving tray and returned to his seat.

The next item of business was the For Sale sign that went up on the house next to the church. The old argument was that St. Michael's was landlocked. The new sign had brought this item to the agenda. Ganshert immediately raised his hand and motioned to table the item. Just as fast, it was seconded. The motion passed without hesitation or discussion.

Father Bernard shot his eyes to the ceiling and lifted up a brief prayer.

The last item to be discussed was the poor attendance at Mass. Once again everyone had good ideas, but no one was willing to take it on, do some research and bring back possible solutions.

Kevin Larson volunteered to do the closing prayer. Normally, Father Bernard would do the prayer, so everyone was surprised when Larson volunteered. After the short prayer, the members quickly got up and hurried to the bathroom.

Now, as Father Bernard walked along the sidewalk enjoying the fresh air, several church members honked their horns and waved enthusiastically as they passed him. He always waved back even when he couldn't see who was in the car.

Once on the square, he walked past the Blumen Keuner Shoppe and stopped to enjoy the flowered window display. Mrs. Brown's colorful flowers were beautiful. The square was busy with people who greeted one another with practiced ease. He felt the tension leaving his body.

Just as he was about to enter the Coffee Bean, an elderly man came out. The wonderful, delicious aroma of fresh coffee wafted out the door onto the sidewalk.

He knew immediately what he was going to order when he stepped inside. From behind the counter, the friendly, dark-haired woman wearing a white uniform smiled at him. Sara always wore her name tag.

"The usual?" she asked.

Father Bernard nodded, and Sara poured him a steaming cup of hazelnut coffee in a large ceramic mug. Even though he had already eaten too many chocolate chip cookies, the temptation for a Danish pastry was too great. He paid for the coffee and pastry and thanked her. He surveyed the café; only about half of the tables were taken. All the ones by the window overlooking the square with a view of the court house were gone. No surprise there.

Toward the back of the customer seating area, he spotted Diane Fouts, the woman he encountered praying at the church. She sat alone sipping a cup of coffee. She was staring at the table as if in a meditative state. He decided not to interrupt her and chose a table next to a mother with a child perhaps five or six years old.

The blue-eyed child pointed to his clerical collar as he sat down and that prompted an immediate conversation. The mother told him that she was from Reedsburg, Wisconsin, and was in Monroe today to buy some Swiss lace. She asked if he knew Father Steve, her parish priest. Both priests knew one another, and that led to a very delightful conversation. The one thing Father Bernard really liked about his vocation was the notion of church family and community and how comfortable he was talking to this visitor. He felt as though he had known her his whole life.

Suddenly Father Bernard felt a light tap on his shoulder. He looked around and saw a smiling Julie Stryker looking down at him with a cup of coffee in her hand.

Julie was a regular at St. Michael's. She volunteered a lot of her time to the church and seemed to thoroughly enjoy her friends there. Since coming to Monroe from Colorado a few years ago, she had gotten a divorce from her husband who betrayed her with another woman. He committed adultery in the eyes of the church. Everyone at the church liked her, and she had the enviable reputation of being very nice and a good listener.

After they exchanged greetings and introductions from the Reedsburg visitors, Julie made her way to the table where Diane Fouts was sitting. Diane got up, and the two women hugged and then sat down. They began to speak in low voices.

After the Reedsburg people left, Father Bernard couldn't help but stare at the two women in the rear of the café. They were totally engrossed in conversation with one another and seemed to ignore the rest of the patrons. He saw Diane reach up and touch her neck. Julie gave her a tissue to dry her eye.

The priest's imagination was getting the better of him. He also needed to get back to the church. He picked up his empty coffee cup and pastry plate and walked over to the women to say good-bye. As he drew near to them, he heard Diane say with resentment, "That Dr. Buckle was a vile man!"

Suddenly both women felt his presence and stopped talking. Diane blushed.

"I just came to say good-bye," Father Bernard said.

They exchanged brief pleasantries. He returned to the front of the shop and left his cup and plate with Sara. He glanced back at the women as he exited the café. On his walk to the church, the priest pondered what he had just witnessed. He was once told by another priest that every human being is constituted to be a profound mystery and a secret to everyone else. Father Bernard considered himself a keen observer of human behavior. What mystery did Diane Fouts hold?

CHAPTER 11

It was seven thirty when Sam entered the squad room at the PD on Monday morning. The first shift officers were out on patrol, so she was alone for the moment. Sigenthaler was to join her at eight to catch up and review the facts of the case. She had time to reflect on the phone calls she had received the night before.

Chief Johns was still at his conference in Washington D.C.; nevertheless, he had called Sam at home last night for updates. She filled him in the best she could. He thought an interview with Dwayne Burkhalter was essential. He found the confrontation in the hospital parking lot with Dr. Buckle interesting. Also, he thought Ingrid Lindquist's response to the news of her husband's death peculiar. He told Sam he felt that she needed to be treated as a person of interest. But then he couldn't understand why a married couple like the doctor and his wife had different names. They obviously were not from Monroe.

After Sam hung up from the chief, Janet called. She had mildly scolded Sam for not staying in touch, not even a phone call. Once again, Janet reminded Sam that when she gets all wrapped up in a case all her friends are immediately on hold. Then she sarcastically asked Sam if she remembered a Drew Nelson? Sam took a deep breath. Oh shit! she thought.

Janet said Drew had tried to call her home in Monroe, but the phone went unanswered. He didn't want to call the PD, so he asked Janet to call to see if she was okay. Sam promised that she would call Drew, and then, for the next fifteen minutes, told Janet about her visit with her mother and how well things were going at the nursing home. Before they hung up, Sam also promised to stay in touch.

Sam had spent the remainder of last evening thinking about her

56

relationship with Drew. He was a really nice guy and never asked intrusive questions about her job or her past. Their time together was both relaxing and fun. He made her laugh. The sex was pretty good. So why did she cast Drew off so easily and quickly after the murder of Dr. Buckle? To be honest, she hadn't given him a second thought once the investigation began. The murder had energized and consumed all her attention. She also realized that her passion to solve the case was at a fever pitch.

Was the graveside promise to Earl to find his killers a mistake? What was driving her obsession? The years were slowly passing her by almost unnoticed. Janet once asked her when she would go from being single to unmarried. At thirty-three, the question began to haunt her. Was she standing in the way of her own happiness? The emotional barriers she built against men over the years had walled her in. She was a prisoner of her own making.

Drew, however, was different. She thoroughly enjoyed being around him. He was funny and a very good listener. He wasn't judgmental when she shared some of her life experiences. She didn't feel threatened by him. Was he just a good friend or was there something else? Could the relationship become serious? Would she have to change? Were they good friends, lovers or what? Was she willing to give it a go and commit to Drew on some level to find out if she could love him? Would he love her back?

All these questions needed to be answered. But then, suddenly, an old friend came back to invade her thoughts. Good old Mr. Insecurity and self-doubt appeared!

Was Drew only something to do between murder cases? The thought of it made her anxious. What does that say about me? she thought as she closed her eyes.

Soon all these unanswered questions had her pacing the room. Love should be easy, but the challenges and passion for her job made it difficult. Suddenly Sam stopped. A thought that made her heart race popped into her mind. It was a serendipity moment. It came from a sudden, visceral sensation in her stomach. Sam realized she had feelings for Drew! For the first time in her life, she instinctively felt that she may have a chance for love; someone to share her life. She instantly felt both excited and scared!

Sam immediately picked up the phone. She held the receiver in her hand and stupidly stared at it. Oh, my God! She had forgotten his phone number. She opened her purse and rummaged around for the slip of paper he had written it on. After a few seconds she found it. She nervously dialed the phone. It rang about eight times before she hung up. Where could he be? She vowed to try again tomorrow to set up a date to see him.

Sam's reflections were brought back to the present moment when she heard Sigenthaler's footsteps on the linoleum floor as he approached the squad room. She hurriedly retrieved an easel and a chalk board from the back of the room and positioned them next to her desk. She then wrote Dr. Buckle's name in the middle of the board with a circle around it.

Sigenthaler wasn't in a very good mood as he made his way down the hallway. He had just come from another argument with his wife about the long hours he was putting in. Becky was canceling prearranged activities like birthday parties with their family and friends. She was furious and frustrated. When the boredom and routine of police work kept her husband on a regular schedule, she was happy. It made running the household much easier. But now she seldom saw him, and when he was with her he was preoccupied with his thoughts. She instinctively knew that his loyalties between the PD and his family worried him. But even knowing that his career came first, she was still unhappy. To help ease the tension she offered up some subtle suggestions for sex that went unanswered.

Their teenage son, Tim, was causing trouble. Being fifteen and acting out was a challenge for the family. With his dad away from the house, his behavior became more exaggerated, and Becky found her patience wearing thin. It was the little things that were getting on her nerves. Tim would snack between meals and leave dirty dishes stacked in the sink for her to wash. In the bathroom, when he finished with a roll of toilet paper, he refused to change it. In spite of all her reminders, he always left lights on throughout the house. His mood swings seemed to range from annoying to defensive to defiance. His attitude was one of entitlement. When he didn't get his way, he got depressed and wandered aimlessly around the house.

Becky understood his rebellious adolescent attitude. Tim wanted independence from his parents. But with her husband being gone so much when she needed him, the atmosphere around the house was getting insufferable. All the adolescent back talk was grating on her nerves. She needed her husband at home more to get back to her daily routine!

As Sigenthaler entered the squad room, Sam noticed a mug of coffee in his hand. He made his way to his desk and sat down. He looked at the chalk board and then to her.

"Good morning," he said. Sam sensed the tension in his voice and returned the greeting. He took a sip of coffee and sat quietly waiting for Sam to begin.

"Rough morning?" Sam asked.

"Don't ask," he replied.

Sam filled him in on her talk with Chief Johns the previous night. She was standing at the chalk board beside her desk, about five feet from Sigenthaler.

"Let's review what we know," she began. "Dr. Buckle was killed some time around eight p.m. the night of the storm. A witness thinks she saw a man dressed in cowboy attire enter the Country Club parking lot across from her house. She isn't sure about the time. The unknown man was wearing a slicker and cowboy hat. From the foot prints that we took, we think the killer is between five-eight and five-nine." Sigenthaler nodded.

Sam wrote the word 'cowboy' on the chalk board and circled it. Then she drew a straight arrowed line from 'cowboy' to Dr. Buckle.

"From our interview with Dr. Ingrid Lindquist, we know that Dr. Buckle had a run in with a man named Dwayne Burkhalter. This occurred in the parking lot at the hospital. We have also learned that Dr. Buckle may have sexually assaulted a Rita Steffes, who was Burkhalter's girlfriend. This incident also happened at the hospital."

Sam wrote the names Burkhalter and Steffes on the board and circled them both. She drew a straight line between them and then she drew a straight line to Dr. Buckle forming a triangle.

"I overheard a conversation at the nursing home that suggested that Dr. Buckle may have assaulted another woman at the hospital. Did any of your interviews mention that?" Sam asked.

Sigenthaler retrieved a note pad from his shirt pocket and looked over his notes as Sam waited. He had spent several hours at the hospital interviewing and gathering information. Then he spoke.

"No one mentioned the possibility of another woman. And you are right. This assault or whatever it was on Rita seemed to be common knowledge. Several people commented on it." He stopped and looked up at Sam. She nodded and he continued.

"This Dr. Buckle had quite the reputation. Other than being a world class heart surgeon, the general opinion was that he was also a world class ass!" Sam laughed.

"These comments came from a few nurses who knew him, as well as some other staff people," Sigenthaler said. "Their take on him was that he was a jerk. The doctors I interviewed only commented that he was a very good surgeon, and other than that they didn't know him every well. He had a tendency to keep to himself."

"Did you interview anyone who might have had any idea who the killer might be, perhaps someone who had a grudge against Dr. Buckle?" Sam asked.

Sigenthaler shook his head. "No one had any names to offer up."

"How about Burkhalter? Did you learn anything about him?"

"The parking lot incident was no secret. It seems that Rita is quite the 'drama queen.' Well anyway, Burkhalter is a piece of work. He is mostly known for his prowess as a bar fighter. We have arrested him a couple of times for disorderly conduct and intoxication. We also picked him up once for drunk driving. I think we definitely need to interview him."

Sam nodded in agreement. "What do you think about Dr. Lindquist? The chief thinks that she should be a person of interest."

Sigenthaler leaned back in his chair and looked at the ceiling.

"It just doesn't fit," he said. "They haven't been in Monroe all that long. Unless the killer is someone from their past, I really can't see her being involved. And besides, what would be her motive? There are thousands of unhappy married couples living in the United States who don't go around killing each other."

Sam agreed. After some more discussion, they planned to interview Rita as soon as they could. After her interview, they would then interview Dwayne Burkhalter.

As they left the room, they both looked at the names on the chalk board and the lines connecting them. Was there a story here or not? They needed more facts!

CHAPTER 12

Rita Steffes sat alone in her one bedroom apartment on 9th Street waiting for Detective Gates and Captain Sigenthaler. The apartment had a new olive green shag carpet. The carpet was an upgrade that was promised by the owners last year. Rita's persistence and nagging finally paid off. A cream-colored macramé plant hanger was home to a philodendron. It was hanging in the corner next to the patio door.

She was sitting in a Lazy Boy recliner drinking a Coca-Cola, smoking a cigarette and looking out the patio door. From where she sat she would see them coming up the sidewalk. Sam had called to set up the appointment. She told Rita that they were investigating the murder of Dr. Buckle and had a few questions for her. Since Rita got off her shift at the hospital at three, the appointment was made for four.

After her shift that day, Rita went straight home and took a shower. While toweling off she looked at herself in the full length mirror that hung on her bathroom door. She had shoulder-length black hair and green eyes. She was five-eight with a slender build. As she stared at herself, she was pleased at what she saw, except for one thing. She hadn't inherited her mother's big boobs. For some genetic reason that she didn't understand, she was rather flat chested with childlike breasts. She wore a padded bra to cover up this defect, but it made dating difficult for her. She often would joke about the size of her boobs when making love, but it seemed to bother her more than her dates.

She decided to dress casually for the interview and pulled on a pair of faded blue jeans and a red polo shirt. She pulled the collar up on her shirt to cover the slight discoloration on her neck. She slipped on a pair of leather sandals showcasing her brightly red-painted toe nails. After brushing her wet hair, she went to the kitchen and opened the bottle of Coca-Cola.

Rita's mind was racing. She was sure that the police had heard about her encounter with Dr. Buckle. Why else would they want to talk to her? What would they ask her, and what would she say about it? And the fact that she goaded Dwayne into confronting the doctor in the parking lot probably needed explaining.

As she waited she couldn't sit still, so she got up and walked around the living room. She decided that the two officers would sit on her living room sofa. Should she offer them some refreshments?

Rita sat down again, and her thoughts drifted to Dwayne. She was really angry with him after one of her girlfriends told her that he was cheating on her. That Dwayne is really stupid! Doesn't he know how fast malicious gossip travels from woman to woman in Monroe? So, by telling him about Dr. Buckle in her most melodramatic fashion, she was hoping that there would be an altercation between them. But that didn't happen. Dwayne totally wimped-out during his exchange with the doctor. Even the gun that he carried in his belt to intimidate the doctor didn't work. For all his bold bravado, he proved himself a coward in the end. She was furious with him!

In fact, the more she thought about his cheating on her, the angrier she became. His dalliance with a creature that was no match for her was especially horrid! She was humiliated in front of her girlfriends. The implication was that she couldn't satisfy him. Rita just couldn't let it go. No guy had ever cheated on her before, and she vowed revenge.

She was now pacing around the room.

The more she pondered these thoughts, the more anxious she became. Was she now somehow implicated in the murder? Perhaps she should have gone to the police after the murder was reported. After all, the rumors and gossip about her had spread like wild fire throughout Monroe. Also, she had avoided Sigenthaler at the hospital when he was interviewing the doctors and medical staff. Did that seem suspicious? The police must have found out something about her flirting with the doctors and Dr. Buckle in particular. What did that say about her?

She sat down again in the Lazy Boy.

As Rita sat sipping her coke, she recalled her first meeting with Dr. Buckle. His reputation as a world class surgeon was the talk of the hospital. It all started in the hallway on the second floor. She accidentally bumped into him and apologized with a childlike grin. He was very nice about it, and they had a brief conversation. The next time she saw him, he stopped her and they chatted. Before she knew it, all this talking moved to flirting. She couldn't believe it. She had flirted with single doctors before hoping to land a husband, but this was happening way too fast. She knew he was married, but then she fanaticized that she may have a fairy tale ending to her life in the works.

The lines between doctors and nurses were well-defined. Doctors were superior! They had the education and hard knowledge to make sick people better. The role of the nurses was all about easing the patient's experiences of suffering and medical invasion. But the real power over the patient was always with the doctor, because he was always held in medical awe. He was the conduit to medical knowledge.

It didn't matter that the nurses thought some of the doctors as rude, dismissive or belittling. The doctors knew who they were in the scheme of things. They were men of science and not to be questioned. The nurses had learned to adapt and accept this hospital hierarchy, because, in the end, the patient's well-being was to be attended to and respected.

The surgical nurses who worked with Dr. Buckle couldn't stand him and his arrogance. The fact that Rita seemed to have his number and his attention grated on some of them. One nurse who Rita didn't know very well cautioned her about Dr. Buckle, but she ignored her concern as jealousy. It turned out that the nurse was right.

Suddenly, Rita noticed the two police officers coming up the sidewalk, a man and a woman. She jumped up, put out her cigarette and greeted them at the door.

After the introductions, Rita seated them on her sofa and asked if they wanted anything to drink. They both declined.

Before they arrived, Sigenthaler agreed that Sam should take the lead during the interview. He felt the questions and conversation would flow better if it was more woman-to-woman. Besides, Rita had avoided him at the hospital.

They both noticed that Rita seemed very nervous. She was fidgeting in her chair. Her hands were in continuous motion touching her face and arms.

Sam started the conversation and explained the reason for them being there. Because Rita's name came up during the hospital interviews as knowing Dr. Buckle, they needed her help in their investigation.

Sam's calm voice and demeanor seemed to put Rita at ease. She stopped fidgeting. Rita relaxed enough to tell them about the flirting and thinking that the doctor was interested in her.

After she finished speaking, Sam asked her about the assault. Rita immediately reached up and touched her neck.

"Well, it happened so quickly. We were alone in the hallway on the second floor of the hospital near the linen storage room. We were chatting like normal. I was working a double shift, and it was about nine thirty p.m. Suddenly, Dr. Buckle grabbed my hand and led me into the dark linen room on the west side of the hospital. The only light in the room was coming from a street lamp outside the window. At first I thought the only reason for his behavior was that he wanted to kiss me. You know, junior high school stuff. I had fanaticized about kissing him, so I was more than willing." As Rita talked, she stared at her feet.

Sam noticed Sigenthaler rolled his eyes.

"Then what happened?" Sam asked.

"As he was about to kiss me, he shoved me against a table with some white towels on it, and then he suddenly lifted me and my butt to the edge of the table. He held me down and with one hand on my neck and reached up under my uniform and ripped down my panties. I was in shock. I didn't know what to do. When he penetrated me, it hurt like hell. But then it was over in an instant. He stood up and apologized and said he was sorry. Then he said he didn't know what came over him. He had never done anything like this before. He reached into his pants pocket and took out five twenty-dollar bills and handed them to me and left the room without another word. Can you imagine? One hundred dollars in cash money!"

They all sat in silence for a few moments.

"Did you report this to anyone?"

Rita looked up at Sam. She hesitated.

"No, I didn't." Her answer just hung in the air. She continued.

"Look, I figured that he lost control of his feelings. From my experience, guys do that all the time when they get excited and horny. Well, anyway, we did it. Screwing a world class heart surgeon was great. I also thought it would be much better the next time we did it."

"Did you do it again?"

"No," replied Rita in a softer voice. "The next time I saw him, he ignored me. At first I thought maybe he was a little embarrassed about the way he acted in the linen room. I tried to talk to him, but he brushed me off. Then he told me to stop bothering him."

"What did you do?"

"It was then that I realized that he used me and that really pissed me off. I told Dwayne, of course. I didn't care if he was some uppity doctor. He wasn't going to get away with it!" Her face was flushed when she finished speaking.

"Was that the last time you had any contact with him?" Sam asked.

"Yes."

"Did Dwayne tell you about the parking lot incident?"

"Yes, he told me." Rita paused.

"And then what?" Sam's question hung in the air for a while.

"I jumped all over Dwayne for not beating him up. Dwayne is a good bar fighter, and for him to wimp out like that was disgusting!"

"Do you know of anyone who might have had a grudge against the doctor?"

"No one that I can think of," Rita replied.

"To your knowledge, did Dr. Buckle ever assault another woman at the hospital?"

"I heard a rumor along those lines, but I have no idea who that may have been. I was having enough troubles of my own."

The conversation stopped for another short pause. No one said anything.

"Just one more thing," Sam asked.

"Where were you on the night of the big storm when Dr. Buckle was being murdered?"

Rita hesitated. Do I tell them that Dwayne was here with me and he was afraid of violent storms? For such a macho man, he is really is a wimp!

"I was here all alone. I heard about the storm at work, so when I got home, I decided to wait it out. The dark clouds and the drop in air pressure were very noticeable. The lighting and the ear splitting thunder put on a noisy display."

Sam looked over to Sigenthaler.

"Do you have any questions?"

He stared back for a moment and then shook his head. No questions.

Sam got up and thanked her for the meeting. She told Rita that they would call her if they had any more questions. And, if she thought of anything else that would help the investigation to call them at the PD. Then Sam and Sigenthaler excused themselves and left.

As Rita watched them go back along the side walk, she looked down at her painted toe nails. I need to call Dwayne, she thought.

CHAPTER 13

Father Bernard's mind was racing as he briskly walked along 20th Avenue toward the downtown square, about a fifteen-minute walk. It was another warm and sunny day in Monroe, eighty-two degrees with light southwesterly winds. There wasn't a cloud in the deep blue sky. As he marched along, he didn't notice the squirrels chasing one another around the terrace trees. He ignored the sweet summer bird songs. The purpose for his trip to the Blumen Keuner Shoppe was etched in his mind and resolve.

After Mass on Sunday, he had briefly talked to Captain Sigenthaler and his wife. More than the usual friendly greeting, he wanted to learn about the murder case and how the investigation was going. The police were keeping it pretty hush-hush, and other than some speculation by the locals, no one seemed to know anything. For Monroe, this was fairly unusual. Keeping a secret from a priest in a small town was next to impossible.

As they chatted, he couldn't contain himself any longer and came right out and asked Sigenthaler how the investigation was progressing. Sigenthaler's wife opened her mouth as if to say something and closed it again. She narrowed her eye brows and instantly looked away. She seemed irritated. Sigenthaler told the priest that he was spending a lot of time working on the case and couldn't talk about it. From their body language, Father Bernard could see the tension between the couple. He offered up a suggestion that, if Sigenthaler needed to talk to someone, he would be available. Sigenthaler eyed him suspiciously. He thanked the priest and assured him that it wouldn't be necessary.

Then suddenly Father Bernard fired a question at Sigenthaler. He didn't think it through before he asked. The question just exploded out of him. He asked Sigenthaler if they were getting close to finding the killer. Sigenthaler's head spun around. That was the wrong question to ask! Sigenthaler shot him a look that was unmistakable: Butt out, priest! He abruptly grabbed his wife's arm and turned and left the priest standing on the front steps of the church. Sigenthaler tried to hold hands with his wife. She jerked her hand away.

Later that afternoon Father Bernard was back at the rectory. He was obsessing on the murder, and it was consuming him. His need to know was driving him crazy. Who was the murderer? The local gossip had the killer as someone living in Monroe. But who could it be? People were being extra cautious about going out at night. They seemed to be looking at their neighbors differently. A dark cloud of suspicion and fear was hovering over Monroe. All the locals were looking for an arrest very soon, so they could relax and talk about the killer.

With all this consternation, Father Bernard was having trouble sleeping at night. Sometimes he couldn't fall asleep until two a.m. With the murder occupying his thoughts during his sleepless nights, he was having difficulty concentrating on his job during the day. Ministering to his flock and socializing with friends was becoming a challenge. Throughout his waking moments, his thoughts never strayed too far from his burning desire to know the truth. He somehow felt he owed it to himself and his congregation.

His chance encounter with Diane Fouts at the church still niggled at him. What was she praying about? What dark secret was she hiding that she couldn't share with her priest? The bruise on her neck had a story to tell, and he had developed an insatiable urge to find out what it meant.

However, he did solve the puzzle of the other woman Diane needed to talk to. After seeing Julie Stryker at the Coffee Bean Café huddled and whispering with Diane, she was the obvious answer. Julie had the reputation of being everyone's good friend. She had a gift for confidentiality and not gossiping or sharing other people's secrets. It was an admirable trait, and she was respected for it. When he causally approached their table, he overheard Diane mention Dr. Buckle's name. When they noticed him, they immediately stopped talking. He wanted so badly to engage them in a conversation about Dr. Buckle, but couldn't think of a way to do it without appearing intrusive. So they just exchanged the usual greetings and smiles.

His imagination was getting the better of him as he sat and dwelled on the murder. He was rewinding and looping the facts as he perceived them in his head. The continuous loop consisted of Dr. Buckle being murdered, Diane Fouts praying in the church with bruises on her neck, Captain Sigenthaler being tight-lipped about the case and the mention of Dr. Buckle's name in the presence of Julie Stryker. He needed to find out and devised a plan to visit Julie Stryker at the floral shop. He knew that the owner, Mrs. Brown, would be in Madison today.

From where the priest stepped onto the square, it was a short walk to the Blumen Keuner Floral Shoppe. Several tourists passed him on the sidewalk and nodded to him. His clerical collar always gave him away. He stopped outside the shop and looked at the flower arrangements through the display window. An elderly lady came out. He held the door for her and then entered.

Once in the shop, he heard the soft sound of a bell attached to the door announcing him. Immediately he was overwhelmed by the strong fragrance of lilies and stock. Father Bernard could identify the lilies, but he didn't have a clue what to call the flowers with that unmistakable clove-like scent. Must be preparing funeral arrangements today, he deduced to himself as Julie Stryker emerged from a room in the back.

"Hi, Father," she greeted him with a smile. "What brings you here today?"

Father Bernard smiled back with his relaxed signature trademark smile and walked toward her. They met at the cash register.

"I was just passing by and decided to stop in and chat with Mrs. Brown. It is such a beautiful day, and I needed some exercise."

"Well, Mrs. Brown is in Madison for the day. Is there anything I can help you with?

"The fresh cut altar flowers delivered to the church every Sunday for Mass are always so beautiful. I wanted to stop by to thank you. We always get compliments on them."

"Thank you very much. I will be sure to tell Mrs. Brown your kind words."

There was a pause in their conversation. Julie was busy and had a couple of arrangements that needed to be finished by four. She thought it odd that the priest just stood there not saying anything.

"Is there something else, Father?"

"Well, yes. I was wondering how you were doing?"

The question caught her by surprise. As far as she was concerned, her life was good. She was keeping busy at the floral shop, and she was enjoying her volunteer work at the parish.

"Why do you ask?"

Suddenly the doorbell rang out announcing a visitor. They both turned to see who it was. Mary Tollakson from the First Christian Church entered. After the greetings were finished and the weather discussed, Father Bernard moved to the far end of the shop and pretended to look over some floral arrangements.

"I heard that Mrs. Brown is in Madison today," Tollakson said.

"Yes, she will be back later tonight."

"I don't know if you read the obituary in the Monroe Press yesterday, but Ida Schwartzlow died at the age of ninety-six. Her funeral is to be at the church, and the family asked Pastor Carl if the church would take care of the flower arrangements. So that's why I am here. Pastor Carl was really impressed with the tall sprays of gladioli, spider mums and carnations you did for the Albert Ammon funeral, so he would like something comparable. Of course, pinks and lavenders would better suit Ida than the reds and yellows you had for Albert."

"Oh, yes, I agree with you." Julie said. "The flowers for the Ammon funeral were wonderful! I will speak to Mrs. Brown, and I am sure the Schwartzlow family will be very pleased."

The two women spoke about the funeral arrangements, flower delivery times and how everyone at the Parkview Nursing Home loved Ida. She had been a volunteer there for twenty years before she became a resident. Pastor Carl was expecting over a hundred people at the funeral.

During this extended conversation, Father Bernard was getting impatient. He had questions that needed answers! He suddenly realized that he was pacing back and forth looking out the window onto the street. The two women seemed to ignore him. Finally, Mary Tollakson bid her farewell and left. She waved to Father Bernard on her way out.

The priest quickly returned to Julie. He picked up the conversation where it had left off.

"The reason I asked you if you were okay was that, when I saw you and Diane Fouts at the Coffee Bean Café, it appeared to me that something was bothering you."

Julie immediately had an eerie feeling. Maybe uncomfortable was a better word. Was she being surreptitiously observed? She just stared at the priest. Just what are you up to, Father? she thought.

As she paused and thought about her answer to the priest, the doorbell rang out again. It was becoming a very busy day at the Blumen Keuner Shoppe. Mrs. Zimmerman, a St. Michael's parishioner, entered the shop.

She was a very sweet, gray-haired lady with a reputation for very long conversations in which she did ninety percent of the talking. About every excuse invented by mankind had been used to politely excuse oneself from her when one's patience ran out.

Mrs. Zimmerman immediately hugged Julie and Father Bernard. He rolled his eyes toward heaven and sighed. Then she proceeded to tell them about her anticipated forty-fifth wedding anniversary and all the details going into the preparations to make the event an exact re-creation of her wedding day. Julie and Father Bernard shared a wide-eyed glance, knowing how impossible that would be. For one obvious detail, Mrs. Zimmerman had long ago surpassed the size fourteen of her wedding dress. Curious as they were, neither of them dared to ask what she was planning to wear, for fear of prolonging her monologue. Mrs. Zimmerman proceeded with her description of the reception, table seating arrangements and menu.

"Fried chicken, mashed potatoes and gravy was Harvey's favorite then and still is to this day!" Mrs. Zimmerman crowed.

During her discourse, Father Bernard was dancing from toe to toe. He couldn't keep still. All these interruptions were driving him wild. He once again walked over to the window and stared out at the street.

As Mrs. Zimmerman droned on, Julie was also getting impatient. She had to finish her flower arrangements, and the hour was getting late. The non-stop talking was taking its toll. She was finally able to get an order from Mrs. Zimmerman for the anniversary flowers.

"Gardenias, I simply must have white gardenias," she insisted. "I know they are a tropical flower and not easy to get hold of here in Wisconsin. And they are probably quite expensive, but I had the most lovely, fragrant gardenias at my wedding, and I simply must have them for our anniversary! We will need one nosegay for me to hold and a boutonniere for Harvey. He thinks his flower will make him sneeze again, but I'm sure he can manage as well as he did forty-five years ago!"

Julie managed to direct Mrs. Zimmerman on to the table centerpieces when the front door suddenly opened again, and Mrs. Strehlow came in. She and Mrs. Zimmerman hugged.

"I know that Mrs. Brown is out of town today, but could you help me with a flower order for the Optimists Banquet?"

"I didn't know that Mrs. Brown was out of town. Where is she?" piped in Mrs. Zimmerman.

Father Bernard threw up his hands. He couldn't handle it any longer.

He was sweating, and his nerves were shot. He went up to the three ladies and hurriedly bid them good-bye. He then charged out the front door, nearly tripping on the doorsill, and hastily retreated back to St. Michael's.

"Well, that was kind of rude!" Mrs. Zimmerman said as he disappeared from sight.

CHAPTER 14

Sigenthaler and Sam were traveling west on Highway 11. The morning was cloudy, overcast and misty, but the weather forecast predicted sunny skies in the afternoon. It was ten thirty, and they had an appointment to interview Dwayne at the Burkhalter Farm. The farm was located about three miles west of Monroe and then two miles south on Steiner Road. When Sigenthaler called Dwayne the day before to set up the meeting, Dwayne told him that today was his day off from the Leuenberger Brewery and he would meet them at the farm.

As they drove to the farm, Sigenthaler asked Sam if she knew anything about the Burkhalter family. She shook her head. Then he asked her if she would like some background.

"Sure," she answered.

Since his wife, Becky, was a second cousin to the Burkhalters, he had attended many family gatherings. Their immigrant story was well known to the extended family.

As Sam stared out the car window looking at the long, straight precision rows of corn and soy beans, Sigenthaler started his narrative.

"The family's patriarch, Hans Burkhalter immigrated to the United States in the late 1860s from Unspunnen, near Interlaken, Switzerland. He was twenty years old. He fell in love with Wisconsin and its fertile land and abundant bounty. He was able to buy cheap land and homesteaded forty acres right here in Green County. As he signed the documents for the land, family legend has it that he cried and said a silent prayer for his future children and grandchildren. Coming from deplorable political and economic conditions in Europe, the gift of land in America was a blessing."

Sam was silent but he had her attention.

"A year after his arrival to Wisconsin and buying the land, he sent for his fiancée, Mary, who he immediately married once she arrived in America. They were very happy and in love as they started their new life together. In their hearts and minds, they knew that this new land offered up a very bright future for them and their children.

"It was tough going in the early years. As they were carving out a new life in the virgin territory, the indigenous Indians were being purged by the government. The constant rumors of Indian attacks kept them on the ready. They armed themselves, but fortunately never fired a fearful shot.

"The new wave of immigrants from Europe who were homesteading the land understood only too well the plight of the Indians. In the long history of Europe, the slaughter and extermination of races of people for land had played itself out over and over again. They were only too familiar with the inhospitable murderous homeland they left behind. Too many wars and too much suffering were etched in their collective past. So all their hopes and dreams for a new and better life in America was being distilled from the blood of innocents."

"Wow," said Sam. "Where did you hear that? I never heard or learned anything like that in school? We murdered thousands of Indians for their land?"

Sigenthaler nodded.

"Now I need to jump to my side of the family. According to my mother, my Great Aunt Edith was an educated woman. Something unheard of back then when women didn't even have the right to vote. She worked for the government during this purging in the late 1800s. She was only one of a very few women who had any formal education for her generation. Mother told us children stories about her job and her meticulous record keeping of the expulsion of the Indians. She even traveled once to a sight where she saw the bodies of massacred women and children. The horrific stories of soldiers raping young Indian girls were confirmed through her own eyes. She recorded it all in a personal diary.

"The military sanctioned the brutality. The revulsion and the injustice of it all caused her to quit her job. She spent the rest of her life railing against the horror she saw, and she died a bitter and lonely woman at the age of ninety-six. She was a Christian woman, so my family reasoned that must have fed into her frustration and anger of being ignored. That's not to say we weren't good people and Christians, but Aunt Edith seemed to be over the top."

"How did her revelation about the treatment of the Indians affect you? You were only a child when you heard the stories," Sam asked.

"I didn't think about it. I couldn't relate to the pain and suffering of the Indians. All I ever heard was that they were savages and were relocated west of the Mississippi. I couldn't understand the notion that the Indians were banished off the land they loved in a land grab by the government. My mother once told me that there is a temptation to remember old things for too long and there is a time for forgetting. And with that the subject was dropped and dismissed."

Sam just sat in silence trying to absorb Aunt Edith. She was the kind of woman that got involved. She didn't sit on her hands on the sidelines and watch the injustice. At least she tried to make a difference. Sam's immediate thought was that Edith's legacy was to be found in the woman's human compassion for the Indians.

"Well anyway, back to the Burkhalters," Sigenthaler continued. "They quickly adjusted to the weather pattern of cold snowy winters and mild warm summers. The land was fertile, so they planted wheat and flourished in their new home. It was a cash crop that served them well in the early years. When the wheat prices fell, they got into dairy farming. They sent their milk to a local cheese factory on Franklin Road and received good prices. And that's where their milk still goes today. Their attachment to the land has remained strong through the generations."

Sigenthaler slowed as he drove through the intersection at Franklin Road and announced that the Burkhalter Farm would be the second one on west side of the road. As they approached the loose gravel driveway, Sam noticed it was long and lined with tall Norway pine trees. She could see a boxy, two-story white house with a wrap-around porch. Brightly colored summer flowers surrounded the steps and front porch. A red barn with a high-hipped roof and white trim stood about thirty yards south of the house. It had a cupola on the ridge of the roof for ventilation. Attached to the barn were two cement silos with silver domes. West of the barn were a shed and pen for Holstein calves and a couple of out buildings. Sam could see about thirty Holstein cows grazing in the north pasture. I wonder if all those cows have names? she mused.

They stopped, got out of their squad car in front of the house and made their way up the porch steps. Four rockers in need of white paint were on the porch. They noticed that the oak front door was open as they peered through the screen door. Sigenthaler knocked and called out. A woman's voice from inside the house said she was coming.

Pam Burkhalter was of medium height, slightly overweight with premature gray hair. Her hair was tied back into a bun. She wore glasses perched on a pointed nose. She was wearing a checkered cotton dress and a flour spattered apron. She was surprised to see them.

"Can I help you?" she asked as she peered through the screen door.

"Oh, it's you Russ. What brings you here?"

"We're here to see Dwayne. Can you tell him we are here, please," said Sigenthaler.

Pam opened the screen door and looked at them.

"This is Detective Gates," he said. She eyed Sam.

"He isn't here," she said. "He got a phone call earlier this morning and left without a word. He just jumped into his pickup truck and sped down the driveway. Why do you want to see him?"

"We are conducting an investigation, and his name came up. We were hoping that he could help us. Did he tell you we were coming here today?"

"No, he never said a word."

"Did he say where he was going?"

"No."

"What time did he get the phone call?"

All this rapid fire questioning was making her very nervous. Her voice started to shake a little.

"It must have been around eight thirty."

"Do you know who called him?"

"No."

"Do you mind if we come in and ask you a few questions?"

Pam didn't know what to do. All these questions had her befuddled. Russ seemed a little on edge and pushy to her. She felt confused and light headed, but invited them in anyway.

"My husband is in the barn. Should I go and fetch him?"

"No. That won't be necessary. I'll go and get him," Sigenthaler said.

After he left, Pam took Sam into the living room and motioned her to sit on her flowered sofa. The room was big and bright. Even on a dreary day, it had plenty of light coming through the lace curtains. An upright piano sat in the corner. The walls were covered with faded striped wall paper. Family pictures were arranged and hung everywhere. An eight by ten picture of the family in a gold frame sat on the desk next to the overstuffed chair that Pam sat in. Pam noticed that Sam was looking at the picture. She picked it up and held it so Sam could see it better.

"This is Fritz and me with our five children," she said.

"A very nice looking family," Sam said. "Which one is Dwayne?"

"He is the one in the middle. In fact, he is our middle child. My mother used to call him, 'the pickle in the middle.'" Then she laughed.

The look on Sam's face suggested an explanation.

"He was an awkward child, and we had difficulty raising him."

Sam nodded.

"Our two oldest are at college in Platteville. The youngest are attending a FFA convention in Iowa this week."

Sam smiled at her.

"Would you like a cup of coffee? It is fresh-brewed. I was making bread when you arrived, so I need to lose this apron."

"Yes, that would be nice. Thank you."

Pam got up and disappeared into the kitchen.

As Sigenthaler made his way to the barn across the lawn, a yellow female collie suddenly appeared from behind a lilac bush next to a wire clothes line with straight clothes pins. The dog ran up to him and sniffed him. After the inspection, she wagged her tail and followed him to the barn. On the way he noticed some calves in the penned up area near the corner of the barn. Next to the calves were a machine shed and a tool shed. A couple of barn swallows flew past him. The swallows reminded him of a barn owl he watched during his youth growing up on a farm. As he approached the barn door, he saw a horseshoe nailed above it. He had heard that in the early 1900s Fritz's dad placed it there for good luck. Farmers needed all the good luck they could get for bountiful harvests and good prices for their crops.

As he entered the barn, he spied Fritz with a pitch fork in his hand at the other end. His body was moving rhythmically as he worked cleaning up the barn.

The milking parlor had eighteen stanchions with automated milking machines. The overhead milk pipe ran to a cooler near the cream separator. Just inside the barn door, a John Deere tractor calendar was hanging on the wall. The calendar was big and had two-inch squares for the days of the month. Sigenthaler could read different hand-scribbled notes to remember calving, milk pick-ups and weights, and cows on medication. He also noticed sticky fly paper strips hanging near the milk tank that needed changing.

A black, dusty radio was sitting on a shelf near the stanchions. Milking parlors all over Green County had a similar style of radio. At four thirty a.m., the local radio station would broadcast Swiss and other polka music for the early milking. The polka music included such favorites as "Beer Barrel Polka," "Hey, Hey Farmer Gray," "Hoop-Dee-Doo" and "In Heaven there is no Beer." All the farmers agreed that the music increased milk production per cow.

On the floor next to the cream tank was an empty bowl. The bowl was usually filled with milk during milking for the dozen or so feral cats that hung around the barn. Sigenthaler could see a couple of them stretched out on a bale of straw.

The barn smells reminded him of growing up on a farm and the sun-up to sun-down routine of hard work. His family worked the farm seven days a week year round to make a living. They rarely took time off for a vacation. His father loved the farm and all that it offered, but the hard work had taken its toll on him. At age fifty-five he looked seventy. He was stooped over and riddled with arthritis.

For Russ Sigenthaler, the hard work and constant attention to detail wasn't for him. He just couldn't see himself ending each day in a dairy barn. So after high school he worked in a local cheese factory until he joined the police department.

Fritz leaned his pitch fork against the manure wagon he was filling to take a break. He looked around and was surprised to see a visitor at the other end of the barn. He recognized Sigenthaler at once and waved. Fritz was wearing denim coveralls and a faded green and gold Green Bay Packers cap. He looked at his pocket watch. Then he walked to Sigenthaler and reached out his calloused hand. After a few pleasantries, they made their way back up to the house.

On the way, the collie ran circles around them. Fritz noticed Sigenthaler's limp and asked him about his leg. Sigenthaler told him what had happened in the line of duty.

"You have a dangerous job!" Fritz joked.

At the back porch, Fritz took off his four-buckle overshoes and parked them on the wooden steps. He entered the house in his stocking feet and slipped on a pair of slippers. He then went to the kitchen sink and washed his hands. Then they proceeded into the living room and joined the ladies.

After the introductions, Pam got up and retreated to the kitchen. She returned with two fresh cups of steaming coffee and a cheese tray with crackers. Thin slices of smoked beef tongue complimented the light lunch of cheeses. Sam also noticed a small pitcher of fresh farm cream and a sugar bowl. Fritz added the cream and sugar to his coffee. As they settled in, Sigenthaler started the conversation.

"I have to apologize to Pam," he said. "I must have come across as a little rude with my direct questions about Dwayne." Pam nodded and smiled. Fritz looked at her.

"What questions?" he asked.

"We have an investigation ongoing at the PD and Dwayne's name came up. He may have some information that could help us. I called him to set up an appointment to meet with him here today at ten thirty a.m. I was surprised he wasn't home."

"What investigation?"

"The murder of Dr. Buckle," Sigenthaler replied. They all sat silent for a few moments as the words sunk in.

"Well, he lit out of here about eight thirty. He was supposed to help me clean the barn." Fritz paused and then suddenly burst out, "Kids!"

Pam jumped and nearly spilled her coffee.

"And you don't know where he went?" Sigenthaler asked.

Fritz looked at Pam and she shook her head.

"All I know is that he took a phone call, and the next thing we saw was the back of him hightailing it down the driveway. Is he in any trouble?"

"We don't know, and that's why we wanted to talk to him. Do you remember if he was home during that violent storm Thursday night?"

Both parents looked at one another.

"No, he wasn't here. He told us that he was staying in town."

"Do you know where he was staying?"

"Not exactly, but it wouldn't surprise me if he was with that girl, Rita."

Pam rolled her eyes. "That girl has a reputation," she said. "We have warned Dwayne about her, but he doesn't listen."

Sam looked at Sigenthaler. He shifted slightly in his chair.

"Do you know if he has a hand gun?"

Fritz furrowed his eye brows. He was getting very uncomfortable with these questions. They seemed a little too accusatory to him.

"Not that I am aware of. We only have hunting rifles and shot guns here at the farm," he answered. Sigenthaler seemed satisfied with that answer.

"Okay, if you talk to him, please tell him that we are looking for him and to give us a call at the PD."

They both nodded.

As they got up to leave, Pam looked a little flush and stayed seated. Fritz showed them to the front door and bid them good-bye. When he returned, she was crying.

On the way back to the squad car, Sigenthaler pointed to a sealed mason jar sitting on a white round table on the front porch. Sam looked at the jar and then back to him.

"Limburger cheese!" he said with a grin.

CHAPTER 15

Jerome Pagel, the summer intern, was sitting at his desk in the Monroe PD sorting through some papers. From where he was, he could clearly see the dispatcher, Shirley Weiss, sitting at her desk near the front entrance door. As part of her job, she welcomed walk-ins during the day. A bullet proof glass barrier separated Shirley from the visitors.

Shirley was in her early fifties and widowed. She was of average height with gray highlights in her auburn hair. She cut her hair short, so she could quickly brush it out and didn't spend a lot of time primping. The chief appreciated that she was a no-nonsense type person and liked things done in an orderly and timely manner. She was the mother figure around the station and kept the chief and police officers pretty much in line. It was hard for her to believe that she had worked at the station for more than twenty years.

This was not the career she had in mind when she married Clarence Weiss. Growing up on a farm near Wiota, she naturally assumed that she would marry a farmer someday. On her twenty-first birthday, she met Clarence at a dance at Turner Hall in Monroe. He was tall and slim, and had soft baby blue eyes. She stared at him from a distance across the dance floor. When he walked up to her and asked for a dance, she fell in love with him. She immediately knew this was the man she was going to marry.

Clarence farmed with his family near Juda. He was equally smitten with Shirley, and after a year's courtship, they were married in the First Christian Church in Monroe. After their honeymoon at the Wisconsin Dells, they rented a farm south of Monroe on County Road B. Both of their families helped them get started, and life was good. The marriage was a good partnership where they continually talked about running the farm and about finances. They had planned to start a family within three years.

Then tragedy struck. One sunny spring morning, Clarence was in the barnyard getting the cows rounded up and ready for milking. The normally docile bull that always seemed to ignore him suddenly charged when Clarence had his back turned and wasn't looking. The coroner told Shirley that Clarence didn't know what hit him. Death was instantaneous. He did not suffer. She was devastated. All her hopes and dreams were shattered. The love of her life was taken from her. She was too young to be a widow at twenty-four.

After the funeral, Shirley moved back to the family farm and helped her mother. For the first year, she was numb. The family support was loving and wonderful. Clarence lived on in her heart, and there was no medicine that could heal her broken heart. Eventually, her mother talked her into finding a job in Monroe. She found work in a real estate office, but didn't care for it. After a couple years, a friend of hers told her about an opening at the Monroe Police Department. She applied for the desk job and got it. The job turned out to be very good for her. The excitement of police work and getting to know the officers was stimulating.

Shirley went out on a couple of dates. They were mostly set up by friends, but the dating didn't go anywhere. As the years rolled on, the ache in her heart never left her. She told herself that the short time she had with Clarence was the memory that would follow her for rest of her life.

Since Jerome's arrival as the summer intern, Shirley had been very kind to him, whereas he was generally ignored by the chief and the officers. After the first week on the job, he considered the work he was assigned very boring. It was more organizing and filing reports than he would have liked. If Shirley hadn't shared some information on how the PD worked behind the scenes and some of the calls that came in, he probably would have quit. He was quickly learning that police work was fairly routine and non-eventful.

Through some family connections, he was able to get this internship. He was in his junior year at the University of Wisconsin in Madison, majoring in police science. The purpose of this internship was to learn about the inner workings of the PD and write a paper for credit.

Jerome was six feet tall and had small shoulders that made his body appear to be misshapen. One friend told him his body reminded him of a pear. He had a long face and wore black rimmed glasses. He wasn't athletic and took no interest in sports. He enjoyed his school work, because he was good at it. In high school he always wore a pocket saver in his shirt. That alone singled him out as a nerd. He had a few friends but was treated as an outlier by most of his classmates. Being quiet and shy caused him problems when trying to date girls. The only time that the good-looking girls took any interest in him was when he was helping them cram for a test during study hall.

Jerome didn't have that spark of magic or whatever it was that attracted girls. He was usually tongue-tied and didn't generate any excitement. Some girls secretly made fun of him. With his adolescent hormones raging, all he could do was look at the beautiful people and realized the unfairness of it all.

When taking school exams, Jerome always scored in the top one or two percent of his class. His few friends also scored well on the tests, but they were also outcasts from the popular social circles. He didn't need a high IQ to understand that high school can be very cruel.

The Dr. Buckle murder was like a shot of adrenaline going through the police department. After it happened, the murder breathed a breath of fresh air into the stale routine of the PD. The department instantly became a bee hive of activity and noise. All the officers were talking about it, and the chief was being questioned daily by Jake Neuberger from the Monroe Press. When the chief was scheduled to go to a conference in Washington D.C., he wasn't happy about it, and the bad language around the station got louder!

When Jerome asked Detective Gates and Captain Sigenthaler how the investigation was going, they ignored him. At least Gates would say that they couldn't talk about it. Sigenthaler just turned and walked away. It seemed to Jerome that Sigenthaler was pretty stressed out.

Shirley told him that Roger Nussbaum was really on the chief's butt to solve the case in a hurry. Nussbaum's attitude was such that it seemed he blamed the chief for the murder. She felt sorry for Chief Johns. In her opinion, the political pressures of being the police chief were immense.

While all this activity was swirling around, Jerome kept slogging away in his own daily routine of organizing stuff. When his friends or family asked him about the murder, he told them that he couldn't discuss it. He enjoyed the sound of it and made him feel that he was somehow involved.

Shirley told him to tidy up the evidence room and make it a priority. The bullets that were taken out of Dr. Buckle would be arriving soon. That meant that the evidence room door would have to be locked and certain sign-in and sign-out procedures would have to be followed.

The evidence room wasn't much bigger than a coat closet. It had a single light bulb in the ceiling and shelving surrounded the three walls. All the shelves went from floor to ceiling. Boxes of this and that were scattered on the shelves. The room seemed to be a neglected catch-all. All the lost and found stuff that was turned in at the PD was placed on any vacant available shelf space. Once a year, all the unclaimed stuff was supposed to be disposed of. But that hadn't happened since Herbert Hager retired as janitor and all-purpose handy man.

Jerome was busy clearing out boxes and other odds and ends, when he found a sealed evidence bag. It had fallen behind some boxes on the top shelf. The bag contained a single bullet. Written on the outside of the bag was the name Officer Randy Miller. He immediately showed it to Shirley.

"Where did you find that?" she asked.

Jerome told her and asked her if she knew anything about it.

"Well, yes. About fifteen years ago," she explained, "a man from Janesville named Ben Smith came to Monroe to rob the First National Bank on the square. He wasn't too bright, if you ask me. He showed the teller his gun and gave her a note demanding money. She reached under her teller's window and the silent alarm system was immediately set off. As she was filling his bag with money, she engaged him in a conversation. Smith was taken off guard by her friendliness and said he was from Janesville. He thanked her for the money and left the bank. Well, anyway, once outside he was confronted by Officer Miller. He started to run away to only God knows where, when he suddenly turned around and fired a shot at Miller. The bullet grazed him in the leg. When Smith turned around again, he tripped on the sidewalk and fell hard on the cement. While he was down, a couple of citizens jumped him and held him there until the police placed him under arrest and took him into custody."

"Boy, that Smith must have been some kind of a nut! What happened to him?" Jerome asked.

"The bullet that wounded Miller was found, and along with the gun Smith used, placed here at the PD to be used at the trial as evidence."

"Was Officer Miller okay?"

"Oh, yes! In fact, he became a celebrity and was recognized for his heroism."

"What happened next?" Jerome asked.

"Good old Ben Smith pleaded guilty, so there was no trial. He spent five years in prison where he died from a heart attack."

Jerome remained silent, soaking it all in.

"What happened to the gun?" he asked.

"I don't know. After the guilty plea, no one ever asked about it or the bullet. That is, until you asked about it today. Maybe Hager got rid of it."

A call suddenly came in, and Shirley answered it. She was going to be on the line for some time, so Jerome went back to his desk. He started looking through some of the old file boxes. He was clearly excited. He was searching for the case notes on the botched Smith bank robbery. Luck was on his side, and he found them. As he read through notes, a thought occurred to him. He needed to write a paper for credit at the end of his internship. So, the more he thought about it, the more energized he became. An idea was coming to him. Since he was interested in ballistics anyway, why not use this old discarded bullet and the case notes as part of his paper. He was sure Chief Johns would okay his request to send the bullet to the crime lab in Madison for analysis. At least, he hoped so.

He grabbed a note pad and a pencil and started scribbling down some notes. Suddenly, a wild idea came to him. To give the paper more punch, why not send along one of the bullets from Dr. Buckle as well, to compare the different markings. The comparison of bullets between an old case and a new murder had all the trappings of an 'A' grade written all over it. He was very pleased with himself. He couldn't sit still. He got up and started pacing around. All he needed to do was to convince the chief of his idea, once he returned from his conference.

During all his excitement, he suddenly realized that he needed some advice. After Shirley got off the phone, he shared his idea with her. She thought it was interesting. However, she cautioned him that the chief probably wouldn't release Dr. Buckle's bullet. Jerome thanked her and went back to his desk and started to formulate a plan to send both bullets to Madison.

CHAPTER 16

Dwayne desperately pressed down the accelerator of his pickup truck as he raced down his parent's driveway. At the end of the lane, he turned south onto Steiner Road and sped toward County Road B. Rita had just called and told him that the police were looking for him. She said they suspected him of killing Dr. Buckle. He immediately went into shock. He told Rita he was with her the night Dr. Buckle was killed. She had raised her voice and said he wasn't with her and that he was probably drunk and killed the doctor. Dwayne swore at her. She abruptly hung up. He needed time to think!

He was white knuckling the steering wheel as he barely slowed down and drove through the stop sign at Melvin Road. Luckily no one was approaching the intersection. His truck skidded on the gravel road through the hard s-curves-his heart rate matching his desperation and speed. He slowed again at County Rd B and ran the stop sign. His tires squealed as he turned east and gunned his engine, speeding towards Wisconsin Highway 69. As he sped past Honey Creek Bridge, he hardly noticed the Holstein cows grazing near the road. Before he knew it, he had passed Bethel Road. He saw only one other car on the road, and it was headed west.

He needed a place to hide out! Instantly, Uncle Harold's abandoned farm place east of Clarno came to mind. Sliding to a stop at Highway 69, he waited for the traffic to clear. Then he gunned his engine again, headed south and passed two cars. He was going seventy miles per hour when he came to County Road P. Slamming on the brakes, he turned east. Outside of Clarno, he passed the old, red brick school building and the West Clarno Pioneer Cemetery. He slowed down to twenty-five mph as he drove through Clarno. After crossing over Richland Creek on the edge of town, he navigated a series of s-curves and raced to his uncle's farm on the south side of the road.

Uncle Harold had rented the farm's forty acres after the Kottkes retired and eventually went into the nursing home in Monroe. After they died, the Kottke family heirs sold the forty acres, the dilapidated farm house and out buildings to his uncle. Dwayne had been there many times, working the fields and exploring the old farm house, barn and other buildings to satisfy his curiosity. No one ever went there; weeds and overgrown foliage had taken over the place. Harold said that someday he was going to raze the buildings and the surrounding grove of trees and plant corn.

Dwayne's rusted-out, green Chevy pickup truck was easy to identify. It had a tailgate full of bumper stickers and a pair of fuzzy dice hanging from the rear view mirror that Rita had put there. The truck also had a trailer hitch to tow his cousin's boat to Yellowstone Lake in Blanchardville. It was their favorite fishing spot, and Dwayne and his friends spent many hours resting their elbows on the tailgate while drinking beer and swapping fishing stories.

Now that he had a good paying job at the brewery, Dwayne thought about trading in this old rust bucket of a truck for a newer model. But he had grown attached to it. He could do the oil changes and maintenance himself. The old truck had become a part of him. The fact that all his friends constantly insulted her gave him a sense of stubborn importance. In the coldest of winters, his truck always started and got him to work on time. That couldn't be said about some of the newer models.

In minutes he had reached the farm place. He checked his rear view mirror. No one was following him. He began to relax a little, and his thoughts drifted back to Rita.

Dwayne had met Rita in high school. He admired her from a distance. There was some unwritten rule at school that differentiated the town kids from the farm kids. She and her girlfriends lived in Monroe, hung out with the jocks and generally ignored the other guys. Dwayne didn't play sports, because his father insisted he stay home to help with the farm work. His mother's pleadings couldn't dissuade his father on this point.

Anger and resentment slowly built up inside him. To his dismay, the girls he liked in school referred to him as just another farm boy. Rita and her friends came from well-to-do families. They always seemed to have the money to dress well and to go to the fun places. Dwayne was jealous. He definitely felt inferior and shamed when he was around them.

Dwayne's frustrations and anger grew as he progressed through the grades. To vent his anger, he stuffed an old feed sack with hay and straw and hung it in the machine shed. Then he put on a pair of work gloves and, like a boxer, spent hours punching it. When the bag went limp, he would fill it up again and whale the daylights out of it. Dwayne was left-handed, so he developed a self-taught technique to take advantage of his south paw punch. The knockout punch! By his senior year, his farm muscles were well-developed, and he was ripped. He would stand in front of the mirror in his bedroom and admire himself. He was proud of his physique.

Then, suddenly, fate intervened. He was invited to one of the after the football game keg parties. These parties usually started around ten p.m. and were always located in the country at a remote spot on someone's farm. The sight was well hidden from the road. A fire pit gave light and warmth. People could sit or stand on blankets scattered on the ground. Coolers of beer were abundant. Whether the Cheesemakers football team won or lost, the drinking and partying went on until one a.m. Dwayne had heard about these parties, but this one was a first for him.

The night was unseasonably warm for mid-October, so the kids were wearing sweaters or light jackets. As he stood talking to some of his classmates, he spotted Rita laughing. She was drinking a beer and enjoying herself with some of her girlfriends. Dwayne grabbed another beer from the cooler, opened it, and slowly worked his way toward Rita in hopes of speaking to her.

The football team was victorious that night, beating a rival school to finish the season undefeated. The players were ecstatic. They were power drinking beer and acting out. One of the players, a big lineman, six-foot-four and weighing two hundred and forty pounds, made a bee line to Rita. He was drunk. He violently grabbed her and threw her to the ground. Rita screamed. Before anyone realized what was happening, he jumped on top of her and started to pull her slacks down. His hands were all over her. She was struggling and crying, but she was no match for him.

Immediately, everyone went into shock. They just stood frozen and stared. No one was going rescue her from a potential Division One Football Player. All the other football players were afraid of him. If any of them hit him too hard during practice, the offending player suffered his rage. The coaches ignored his behavior. Butch Konkel was big and strong, and he had a mean temper. The moment was surreal. He was attacking Rita in front of thirty or more witnesses.

Suddenly, something inside Dwayne snapped. He raced toward the bully and hit him as hard as he could in the shoulder with his body. The impact knocked Konkel off Rita. He got up and looked dazed. Dwayne jumped up and held his ground in front of him. Rita scampered to her feet and joined the crowd. One of her friends wrapped a blanket around her.

The crowd gasped as Konkel lunged at Dwayne. Dwayne hit him as hard as he could in the stomach. Konkel went down. Dwayne was breathing hard. The adrenaline was madly pumping through his veins. He focused totally on his opponent.

Konkel got up and stared at Dwayne. He looked surprised. No one had ever challenged him like this before. He felt like he could squash anyone who got in his way. "This little bug would be easy pickings," he muttered to himself, and he heard the crowd cheering. That spurred him on and gave him the courage to beat the hell out of this little shit. He laughed out loud, and then he charged Dwayne.

Dwayne quickly side-stepped him and hit him second time in the stomach. The crowd of on-lookers gasped again. The brute went down hard. As Konkel was trying to get up, Dwayne started hitting him, rapid-fire. His two-fisted rage was fueled by raw anger. Images of flailing away at the punching bag in the machine shed raced through his mind. The more he hit him, the better he felt.

But now, Konkel towered over him and was trying to hit back, but he only made glancing blows. Dwayne's fury continued pounding at him, relentlessly, with body blows and face punches. Finally, Konkel went down and lay still. His face was bloodied, and his nose was broken. He was a beaten man.

Dwayne was sweating and breathing very hard. He took his eyes off the prone attacker and looked around. The partygoers were staring at him in disbelief. Then he looked down at his own bloody fists. He was so pumped up, he didn't feel the pain in his knuckles and wrists.

Then the cheering began. Even the football players were impressed. Rita ran up to him and gave him a long, sensuous kiss on the lips. Dwayne was stunned. He stepped back and saw the moonbeams dancing around her smiling face. They made her glow. Dwayne smiled at her and shook with delight. His reputation and manliness were born on that moonlit October night. In the flickering light of the bon fire, a hero was born. He had slapped the school bully in the face!

Fate had given him Rita. The once so distant and unattainable goddess was there kissing him. He had arrived. Dwayne was no longer the outsider.

Unbridled violence defined him. Rita squeezed his bloody hand and whispered that she would properly thank him later. Suddenly, he went from feeling special defending Rita's honor to feeling superior. Something else had happened to Dwayne that night, which he couldn't comprehend. Rita's sensuous kiss under the stars had started him on a journey of desire, passion and betrayal.

The following Monday, Rita announced to the school that she had a new boyfriend. She warned the other guys to stay away from her or she would send Dwayne after them. After that surprising announcement, Rita and Dwayne became a steady couple, much to his delight. When he saw Konkel in the hallway, the former bully would turn and walk away. The new feeling of power was intoxicating.

The hormones in Dwayne were running rampant and went straight to his brain. Having sex with Rita mesmerized him. Suddenly, everything else in his life seemed dull and empty. As he strutted around, he was surrounded by people who laughed out loud at his sorry jokes and giggled at his antics. He actually believed he was something special. Dwayne truly felt he had left one world and was now living in another, a world of privilege. He had upgraded himself.

After high school, Dwayne got a job as a laborer in a local cheese factory. Rita went to nursing school in Milwaukee. After she received her nursing degree, Rita applied for a nursing position at the hospital in Monroe. She made enough money to rent an apartment and to live independently. She continued to date Dwayne with the thought that if something better came along she would take advantage of the opportunity.

Going to school in Milwaukee had changed Rita's perception of boys. The guys she met there seemed worldly to her. They were far more interesting than the guys in Monroe. Her nursing classmates continuously chattered and dreamed about finding a doctor to marry. The prestige and money was the fairy tale ending that they all fantasized about. Perhaps Rita could make her dream come true in Monroe. But for now, Dwayne would do.

Dwayne didn't like the hours or the hard work in the cheese factory. Through some friends he was able to land a job at the brewery. He really liked the better wages and the work. During Rita's absence and schooling in Milwaukee, he became a regular at the Brass Tap Bar on 17th Avenue. It was here that he honed his prowess as a bar fighter.

Dwayne slowed his truck as he came to the driveway of the farm place. The drive was overgrown with weeds. As he turned in and inched his way along to the dilapidated barn, he felt confused and alone. He got out of his truck and struggled against the rusted hinges of the big double barn doors. The hinges finally yielded. He backed his truck into the barn and closed the door. He could see the sky through the holes in the roof.

After Dwayne was satisfied that he was safe from the police, he reached into the glove compartment of his truck and took out the .38 Special. He stared at it for several moments. He then exited the barn and slowly walked over to an abandoned well located about twenty feet from the house. It was overgrown with weeds and poison ivy. He carefully removed the rotting wooden cover to the well opening and threw the gun down the hole. He didn't hear the splash he was expecting. The well was dry. He replaced the cover and went back to the barn.

Dwayne's cousin, Bob Kraus, worked for Uncle Harold. Part of his job working for their uncle was to drive by the farm place every day to check on it. He often complained to Dwayne that it was a waste of time, but Harold was always fearful that vandals would damage either his crops or his buildings. Harold was well-known for being as tight as tree bark when it came to money, so the constant vigilance on his property didn't come as a surprise to anyone who knew him.

Dwayne and his cousin were close friends. His plan was to wait for Bob to come to the farm place and explain his situation. He was sure that Bob would keep his hiding place a secret and bring him cigarettes, food and beer. Dwayne reasoned that after a couple of days he would have worked out a plan for his future.

CHAPTER 17

Sam made another appointment to visit Ingrid Lindquist. Dr. Lindquist wanted to meet at the hospital, so the meeting was set for four thirty p.m. in her office. Chief Johns was back from his conference, but Roger Nussbaum was taking up all of his time. Johns wasn't too happy about this development. He wanted to be more involved in the case. Sigenthaler had requested to take a couple days of vacation, but Johns denied him the time off.

"There is no time off when investigating murder!" Johns told him. He also told Sigenthaler to find Dwayne Burkhalter.

The investigation wasn't making much headway in Sam's opinion. The eye witness account of a cowboy was interesting, but it got them no closer to the truth. She didn't consider Dr. Lindquist a suspect, but she needed to satisfy Chief Johns. So what about Burkhalter? Sigenthaler thought that he was their prime suspect. But could they trust Rita to tell them the truth? Too many unanswered questions. The mystery woman that Dr. Buckle assaulted interested Sam. She needed to find and interview her. But first she needed to keep her appointment with Dr. Lindquist.

Ingrid Lindquist looked at the clock on the wall in her office. Detective Gates would be there in thirty minutes. Her office was on the second floor of the hospital facing west. It was a relatively bare office containing only a few furnishing. Dr. Lindquist's professional diplomas and certificates were framed and hung on the wall, but no other framed pictures were present to give the office a feeling of warmth. Noticeably absent was a picture of Dr. Buckle. A book case contained only a few books. She had a large wooden walnut desk with two overstuffed chairs facing it. Behind the chairs was an antique fainting couch covered in a dark burgundy fabric. Some of her patients used the couch to lie down on during therapy. It was surprising how many patients didn't want eye-to eye contact when discussing their problems.

Dr. Lindquist sat upright in the soft brown leather chair behind her desk. Her last scheduled patient for the day had left. Looking out the window with the blinds fully open, she could see the bright blue cloudless sky. On her desk sat a vase of freshly cut flowers and a sympathy card from the hospital staff.

It had been a long day. She felt tired. After finishing some paperwork on her desk, she stood up and made her way to the fainting couch. She loosened the belt around her waist, unbuttoned the top button of her skirt and pulled up her flowered cotton shirt from the waist of her beige skirt. She felt instant relief as she collapsed onto the couch. As she lay with her head slightly elevated, she looked down at her feet. With two swift kicks, her shoes went flying toward the middle of the room. Then she stared at her feet as she furiously wiggled her toes inside her nylon stockings. The stress was leaving her body. She crossed, uncrossed and crossed her ankles. The room felt warm to her. She laid her head back on the couch and closed her eyes.

The first patient Dr. Lindquist had seen that day was a woman who had recently lost her baby from crib death. She was grieving and very depressed. Having two other youngsters at home, she kept referring to herself as a "potty mummy." Her next patient was a puffy eyed, young single woman who had a medical diagnosis of Chlamydia, a sexually transmitted disease she got from her boyfriend. The woman felt deeply betrayed. He had sworn his undying love and commitment to her, only to leave after the diagnosis was confirmed. The woman was spending her mornings drinking vodka while lounging around in her in her orange-checked pajamas. She was deeply depressed.

As the hours droned on, Dr. Lindquist saw a steady stream of ordinary people coming to see her to share their most private and intimate thoughts. After all, she was a trained and trusted therapist, so they all trusted her to keep their secrets in the strictest of confidences. At times, during her lighter moments, she felt as if she was watching a striptease artist at work, when listening to her clients. Just like the dancer, her patients would slowly peel off their emotional clothes until the naked truth came out. But then she reminded herself that she was a trusted professional. She fully understood that the counseling she gave her patients was the glue that held their lives together.

After her sister-in-law had left Monroe, taking Dr. Buckle's ashes back to England for burial, Ingrid Lindquist felt alone and agitated. She soon discovered that a good night's sleep was almost impossible. During the night she turned and twisted and punched her pillow with her fist. When sleep finally came, her dreams were filled with terror, abandonment, and the frustration of the unacceptable and the unattainable.

After coming to Monroe, she didn't have any close friends. The people were nice enough, but she didn't connect with them on a personal level. Ingrid needed support and started calling her family in Stockholm. The support she received from them was a welcomed gift. The phone calls comforted her and gave her hope. She decided to sell the house and move back to Sweden. She spoke to the hospital administrator about it and gave her notice. It was agreed that it would take about thirty days to clear her patient calendar. She would leave the house in the hands of a local realtor. At a reduced price, she felt the house should sell fairly quickly.

From the gossip at the hospital, she learned the police were actively investigating the murder. The man who confronted her husband in the parking lot was a suspect. His name was Burkhalter. The name didn't mean anything to her.

The sudden shock of the murder was slowly wearing off. The transition of going from a young wife to a widow was staring her in the face. There was no preparation or final last words. She knew that her marriage wouldn't last, but she never imagined it would end like this. In her quieter moments at home, she would sip a glass of wine and reflect on her marriage. Guinevere was her sole comfort.

When Ingrid first met Dr. Buckle she immediately fell in love with him. She was blinded by the bright light that surrounded him. The aura of his brilliance and his status as a world class heart surgeon overwhelmed her. The special attention he paid to her while dating left her totally in his control. He gave her flowers and expensive jewelry, and took her out dining and dancing. He whispered the passionate words of love that she longed to hear. As far as she was concerned, he "walked on water." He was a powerful man of influence.

Shortly after their marriage, rumors started to circulate. At first she rejected all the mounting evidence that he was unfaithful to her. They had been married less than a year. To her, trust was the foundation of any marriage. But that foundation was crumbling fast. When she confronted him about the affairs, he admitted that they were true. She was devastated. A very dark and hidden personality surfaced in him that she didn't recognize;

a side of him that she didn't know existed. He was no longer the man she fell in love with.

After she confronted him, his behavior toward her abruptly changed. He belittled her in the most shameful and egregious way. The message was clear. He had his trophy bride, and she had no choice but to adjust to his ideas of marriage. She felt ashamed and trapped.

While they were dating and before they married, Ingrid shared with him all the intimate details of her life. She didn't want any surprises. The disclosers included broken relationships and sexual behaviors that she deeply regretted. Dr. Buckle told her in a very kind and understanding way that whatever she did before they met was of no consequence. It just didn't matter. He loved her and that was all that mattered. Hearing those words from the great man only heightened her passion and love for him.

However, Buckle didn't return her trust. He only told her that his past was painful and would not infringe on their marriage in any way. He had his secrets, but she didn't inquire and overlooked that detail. Little did she realize the sheer size of the emotional baggage he was carrying on their wedding day, as they left the church together to share a life of marital bliss.

But all that changed the night he was murdered. Ingrid was initially thrown into the chaos of moment. As the shock gradually wore off, she became rather giddy. A great burden had been lifted from her shoulders. It was a tremendous feeling of relief! Her days of walking on egg shells were over. All that mattered to her now was the exuberant feeling of being free.

The phone suddenly rang in the office. Dr. Lindquist jumped up and told the receptionist to send Detective Gates up in five minutes.

She tucked in her shirt, re-buttoned her skirt, ran her fingers through her hair, and slipped on her shoes. When she heard a gentle knock on her door, she welcomed Sam into the office and directed the detective to one of the high back chairs in front of her desk as she sat down in the other one.

"What can I do for you?" Dr. Lindquist asked with a smile.

Sam immediately noticed a changed woman sitting in front of her. This was not the same person she had interviewed earlier. Dr. Lindquist's features had softened considerably, and she seemed more relaxed.

"I wanted to give you an update on our investigation and ask you a couple of questions," Sam said.

"Okay."

Sam told her about the progress they were making to find the killer. Dr. Lindquist was very quiet and listened intently. Sam was pleased with the interest she was showing. After her briefing, Sam sat back in her chair and relaxed. Then a slight silence followed.

"Is there anything I can do to help?" Dr. Lindquist asked.

"We are still looking for anyone who may have had a grudge against the doctor. Anyone who would do him any harm?"

"You mean other than the man who confronted Dr. Buckle in the parking lot?"

"Yes."

"No, I can't think of anyone. As you know, we are new to the city. Other than a few parties at my house, we didn't socialize much. Dr. Buckle liked to go to Chicago, when our schedules allowed, for the culture and entertainment."

Sam felt she needed to change the direction of the interview. "How are you getting along? Are you feeling okay?" she asked.

Dr. Lindquist told her about her plans to leave Monroe and move back to Stockholm. As she shared her story, she showed very little emotion. Her tone was rather clinical in that she could have been talking about someone else.

"You are probably wondering why I despised my husband," she suddenly said.

Sam sat up in her chair and stared at her.

"At first I was blinded by my love for him. While we were dating, the rumors about his womanizing were fairly well known. But he swore to me that it was all in the past and he truly loved me. I believed him, of course. Shortly after we married, he started cheating on me. The I-told-you-so crowd further humiliated me. I was trapped. His behavior toward me turned misogynistic. So that's the reason you didn't see any tears or lace hankies when he was murdered. I had no more tears to give."

Sam didn't say anything.

"The person who killed my husband actually did me a favor. I know it's a cruel thing to say, but I really feel liberated and free from his control."

Another silence followed. Sam didn't know how to respond.

"I know that all this information may come as a shock to you, and I apologize for that. Other than that Burkhalter person, I have no idea who may have killed him. When you find the killer, I am quite certain he had good reasons." She paused and smiled at Sam.

Sam didn't have any more questions. She thanked Dr. Lindquist for her time and told her that she would be in touch. As Dr. Lindquist walked Sam to the office door, she abruptly stopped.

"Just one more thing, Detective, I did hear something that might interest you."

Sam looked at her.

"The hospital gossip has it that a woman named Diane Fouts may know something about Dr. Buckle. But, of course, this is only tittle-tattle."

"Does she work here at the hospital?"

"Yes, but that's all I know."

Once outside Dr. Lindquist's office, Sam wrote down the name Diane Fouts in her interview notebook. Maybe this is the mystery woman I have been looking for, she mused.

CHAPTER 18

efore going home Thursday night, Sigenthaler spent an hour at the Brass Tap Tavern on 17th Avenue. He needed to talk to the patrons. This was the bar where Dwayne hung out. It was also the place that kept his reputation as a bar fighter going. Everyone there knew Dwayne.

The Brass Tap was located a block off the square and pretty much catered to the locals. It was rectangular in shape with the long bar on the north wall. Behind the bar was a grill for cooking brats and hamburgers. Beside the grill was a French fry cooker that reeked of burnt oil. On the bar was a jar of pickled pigs' feet preserved in vinegar brine. Some smoked beef sausage links were hanging over the bar in their natural casings. Stemmed glassware hung upside down next to the sausage.

The bar itself didn't have very good lighting, so anyone entering from the street had to adjust their eyes to the semi-darkness. Neon beer signs helped the lighting situation. Upon entering the bar, one could see two pin ball machines located on the south wall near the door. Beyond them were several small tables that led to the pool tables and the restrooms. The bar was mostly decorated in faded Green Bay Packer paraphernalia. The smell of stale cigarette smoke and spilt beer greeted all the patrons.

As Sigenthaler entered the bar, Dan Heller, the bartender, waved to him. Heller was fifty-seven and looked older than his age. He was balding and had dark circles around his eyes. The weathered wrinkled skin on his face and neck broadcasted a hard life to the world. He had a second job working for a local landscaper. The only reason the bar owner kept him on was because he was the brother of his wife. What Heller didn't make in wages, he made up in booze. Sometimes, near closing time, he would pass out, so a patron would jump in behind the bar and finish serving drinks. The unusual thing about the Tap was that it operated on the honor system. When the night's receipts were tallied, the cash drawer usually balanced. "Honor among drunks" was Heller's standing joke.

Sigenthaler looked around and saw about a half dozen people. They were sitting at the bar drinking beer and smoking cigarettes. He knew all of them. They greeted him with a nod.

"How's about a beer?" Heller asked as Sigenthaler sat down on a bar stool.

"Sure, why not."

Heller's experience as a drinks mixer was fairly limited. He could handle beer, brandy, vodka and whiskey. He didn't like orders for sweet girly drinks and would often get complaints. A woman visitor from Chicago once ordered a Sidecar. Heller was totally flustered. He had never heard of such a thing. She was already in her cups when she came into the Tap. She gave him a hard time and swore under her breath. Then she boldly walked behind the bar, shoved him out of the way and made her own drink. The bar crowd loved it, and for the next six months everyone ordered a Sidecar. The humor and humiliation was hard to live down.

As Sigenthaler sipped his tap beer, he turned to the folks beside him. He said they all knew why he was there, then he asked them where Dwayne was hiding. A woman with red dyed hair and black rimmed glasses told him in a slurred voice that Dwayne was probably in Alaska. The patrons erupted in laughter.

"Dwayne was always boasting that he would go to Alaska and work the gold fields to get rich," Heller told Sigenthaler. "No one ever took him seriously, because it was the beer that was doing the talking."

"Are you on or off duty?" another patron asked. Sigenthaler ignored him.

"We are looking for Dwayne, because he may have information to help us solve the murder of Dr. Buckle. I think someone here knows where he is." Silence followed. "You all need to take this inquiry seriously."

The patrons looked at one another. They all shrugged.

"I haven't seen him," the redhead said. "Have you talked to Rita? She keeps pretty close tabs on him."

"Have you talked to Bonnie?" asked a man with an unshaven face and two front teeth missing.

"Bonnie?" Sigenthaler asked.

"Yea, Bonnie Koss. It seems that she is giving Dwayne a little side action."

"Shut your mouth!" the redhead exploded.

"Well, it's true."

Sigenthaler just shook his head. He had wasted enough time. He finished his beer and told them to call the PD if they found out where Dwayne was.

The next day Sigenthaler parked his patrol car along 16th Avenue and watched the customers go into Baumgartner's Cheese Store & Tavern. The tavern was located next to the Swiss Colony Bakery on the west side of the square. It was seven p.m. and the sun was setting. He wanted to interview the bartender and the after-supper bar crowd to glean any information he could concerning Dwayne Burkhalter. So far the police couldn't find him, but Sigenthaler was convinced that someone in Monroe knew where he was hiding. From his experience as a police officer, he knew it was impossible to keep a secret in Monroe.

Sigenthaler got out of his patrol car and made his way along the sidewalk to Baumgartners. Just inside the front door, Green County cheeses and sausages greeted him from display coolers along the north wall, with the cash register at the end of the counter. Across the room were several wooden booths for patrons. One young couple was finishing up a meal of barbecue ribs, baked beans, slices of brick cheese and cold beer. The ribs smelled wonderful.

The bar area was in the back, through an arched doorway. The bar itself was on the north wall too and seated about twenty people. The black, high-back bar stools butted up against a brass foot rail. The menu board above the bar highlighted the local cheeses and meat sandwiches that were served. At the east end of the bar, several limburger cheese sandwiches were wrapped up and ready for takeout.

The room was well lit, and waitresses were busy waiting tables. Swiss music played softly in the background. The loud and lively chatter and laughter permeated the evening. Everyone was having a good time.

Sigenthaler took an empty bar stool at the far end of the bar. He noticed a few old-timers playing euchre at the tables near the rest rooms. Surveying the room, he saw many people he didn't know. Baumgartners and the Green County Courthouse were two of the most photographed and recognizable places in the state of Wisconsin. Because of their notoriety, the tourism business was very good in Monroe.

The person he needed to talk to was Adam Polus. He was tending bar tonight and was very busy. Adam was a life-long resident of Monroe and knew just about everybody. Over the years, he had accumulated a wealth of knowledge just talking to people at the bar. He knew all the dysfunctional soap opera stuff around town before the news hit the gossip circuits. He knew who was cheating on whom and which marriages were heading full speed into divorce court. If anybody knew were Dwayne was, Adam had to be the man.

Sigenthaler was surprised to see Sam as she suddenly appeared. He wasn't aware that she was coming in tonight. He asked the guy next to him to move down a chair to make room for her.

"So how was the beer at the Brass Tap?" she asked with a smile.

Sigenthaler grinned back at her. "Does the chief know?"

"Everybody knows!"

"Oh shit!" muttered Sigenthaler and Sam laughed.

"All those people at the Tap are nuts. My questions got either blank stares or stupid comments. I wasted my time there and ended up in the weeds!"

They lowered their voices, and Sam updated him on her activities. She asked if he knew a Diane Fouts, and he told her Diane was the wife of a lawyer in town, named Jeff Fouts. Sam then told him about her conversation with Dr. Lindquist. He agreed; they needed to interview Mrs. Fouts.

"It seems that Dwayne has vanished from the face of the earth," Sigenthaler said. But he assured her that if anyone knew where he was, it would be Adam.

Adam's helper came back from break, so Adam went to the end of the bar to see Sigenthaler, who introduced Sam. He smiled at her.

"Forget it!" Sigenthaler said. They all laughed.

Sam glanced over to the guy in the next chair. He had his back turned and was ignoring them. He was chatting up a woman next to him by telling her it was impossible to drink but one Huber beer, and he had to make an extraordinary effort to stop at two. Then he laughed at his own joke. Sam turned her attention back to Adam.

"Yeah, I think I might know were Dwayne might be," Adam said in a low voice.

"Hey, we haven't even asked you yet." Sigenthaler said.

"Lucky guess, I suppose." Then he grinned and continued.

"Bob Kraus, Dwayne's cousin, comes in and orders limburger cheese sandwiches to go. One day while he was waiting, he struck up a conversation with a tourist who wanted to know something about limburger cheese. Bob told him that he detested the stuff himself, but he was getting it for his cousin. I overheard this while I was fixing the sandwich."

Both Sigenthaler and Sam stared at him, saying nothing. Adam knew he had their full attention.

"I asked Bob how things were going. He started complaining about his low wages and how he needed to talk to his Uncle Harold about them. Then he suddenly said something unintelligible about being a delivery boy. I asked him what he was talking about, and he said his trips to Clarno were becoming a pain in the ass. Then he put his hand over his mouth and left."

"So . . . ." asked Sigenthaler. "What does that mean?"

"It means that Dwayne is hiding at the Harold Burkhalter farm in Clarno!"

Sam coughed and looked at Sigenthaler.

"Oh, just shut up," Sigenthaler said.

Adam looked Sigenthaler in the eye. "The next time I get pulled over for speeding, I want you to remember who the real detective is here in Monroe!"

"Okay, okay, I get your point."

Adam left them and went to wait on a customer.

"Do you know where the farm is?" Sam asked him.

"Yes, I do. I know exactly where it is."

CHAPTER 19

Dwayne sat alone in the cab of his pickup truck, holding a bottle of beer in his hand. He was in his uncle's barn with the doors closed listening to Hillbilly Country music from Nashville. The sun was starting to disappear over the horizon. As the darkness engulfed him, he stared through the windshield of the truck looking at nothing in particular. He was thinking.

The country music relaxed him. He loved this kind of music. He liked the nice melodies and strong lyrics. Most of the songs told a story simple enough to understand and represented real life. His favorites were the ones where boy meets girl, they fall in love and either live happily ever after or break up. Love and heartache were popular themes and touched on the struggles of youth or hitting the road in search of a new identity. He could find himself in the lyrics. Rita hated country music and preferred rock 'n roll.

The days had morphed together since his arrival. He had lost track of the days of the week. He thought it was Friday, but he wasn't sure. It had been several days now since he fled from his parents' home. He was lonely and afraid. His only companions were the birds, squirrels and the occasional deer. He even saw a red-tailed fox. The noises at night were creepy. Even though he locked himself into the cab of his pickup truck at night, he didn't sleep very well.

Every time a car passed the farm on County Road P, he cringed, thinking it might be the police. He didn't know how long his cousin Bob would be able to keep his secret. Every time he came with food and beer he seemed a little crankier. What had started out as a fun adventure for Bob was quickly turning into drudgery.

Dwayne had plenty of time to think about Rita and the trouble he found himself in. It was slowly dawning on him that Rita was really a bitch. The more he thought about Rita, the more upset he got. From the get-go, she had gotten under his skin, and there was no means to escape. Her sugary sweet voice and strong perfume were intoxicating! Looking back on it, the way she treated him was terrible. He now fully appreciated that it was the sex that held them together. It wasn't love! The sex was like a drug. He just couldn't get enough of it. No matter what kind of pain she inflicted on him, he was hooked and needed another fix. Just being around her drove him crazy. She knew how to play him. Her naked body was all the prompting he needed. She was in total control.

His affair with Bonnie Koss was a mistake, and he blamed Rita for it! It started after a bar fight at the Tap. It was one o'clock Sunday morning when the bar was getting ready to close after a Saturday night of drinking. Rita was flirting with some loser from Madison who was buying her drinks. They had been drinking all night, and the guy was getting ideas about Rita. At closing time, he suddenly grabbed her around the waist and started to forcibly take her outside. Rita instantly realized what was happening and called out to Dwayne. He immediately intervened and challenged the opportunist.

The bar crowd instantly became energized and formed a circle. Rita had set Dwayne up like this before, and he always delivered. After all, he was her hero! The problem was this interloper was stronger than he looked and was no stranger to a fight. As he and Dwayne pounded on each other, the blood flowed to the delight of the cheering throng. Cuts to chins and nose bleeds fed into the frenzy of the crowd. They loved the fighting and every scintillating moment of the circus-like atmosphere. The cheering was loud and raucous. The two gladiators went after each other with practiced enthusiasm. When Dwayne scored a direct hit that sent his opponent reeling, the applause and noise from the crowd shook the air again and again.

After a several minutes, Dwayne was getting the upper hand. He landed a solid punch that sent his opponent reeling against a pool table. He laid there sprawled out with his face down in the green felt. The crowd erupted again in cheers. The unbridled violence pulsated throughout the room. Dwayne turned and bowed to the crowd. Another battle, another victory.

Then suddenly, the guy grabbed a pool cue and swung it at Dwayne. It was a direct hit to the head. Dwayne instantly blacked out and went down. He lay unconscious on the floor. Every one shrieked. The guy ran out of the bar, jumped into his pickup truck and sped off.

The stunned crowd just stared in silence at Dwayne as he lay bleeding on the floor. No one called the police. Dan Heller came out from behind the bar to assess the situation. The crowd dispersed and headed for the exit. They were all disappointed and chattered about the unfairness of the fight. No one had ever used a pool cue before, so they declared Dwayne the winner. The other guy cheated.

Rita left with the crowd. Her hero had let her down.

Heller was cleaning up Dwayne's face with a damp bar towel when he started coming to. Behind him was Bonnie. She told Keller she would take over. Keller was relieved, because he needed to clean up the bar, count the cash receipts and go home.

Bonnie was a regular at the Tap. She was blonde, twenty-four-years old and single. She was one of the leftover unmarried women in Monroe. It depressed her. Being five-foot-five and thirty pounds overweight limited her opportunities to find a husband. She was in love with Dwayne, but she never had a chance to prove it. Other than a few dalliances with some of the bar regulars, she only remained a face in the crowd. Tonight she was hoping her luck would change.

When Dwayne became fully conscious, his head hurt like hell. He was lying on the floor looking up at Bonnie. She smiled at him. When he asked her where Rita was, Bonnie told him that she had left the bar with her friends. As he struggled to his feet, he leaned against her for support. He ached all over. His opponent had done a number on him. Bonnie suggested that they go to her apartment to clean up. She only lived about three blocks away on 11th Street. Dwayne was pissed at Rita for leaving him there and agreed. Bonnie was thrilled.

Once in her apartment, Bonnie ran him a hot bath. She gave him a couple of aspirin before he settled into the hot water. The bath was relaxing and felt really great. After a long soak, he toweled off and joined Bonnie in her living room. She was sitting on a flowered sofa in loosely fitting cotton pajamas. The living room lights were dimmed. Her pajama top was unbuttoned revealing a plump pink breast. Dwayne could see her soft, sensuous, seductive smile as she leaned back on the sofa. The sight of her breast and her smile immediately turned him on.

The next morning he woke up in her bed. She made him breakfast. Before he left, she told him that he could have her anytime he wanted to. Rita was angry at him for losing the fight, so he saw Bonnie a couple of more times mostly to spite Rita. When Rita found out about his brief affair with

Bonnie, it ended. Rita went crazy. No one had ever cheated on her before, and Dwayne was going to pay.

He sat thinking about all of this—Rita had indeed gotten her revenge! Dwayne knew he couldn't stay in his hiding place forever. He also figured out that he needed to make a change in his life. If he could only get some money together, he would go to Alaska. Leaving Monroe and Rita behind was his only chance at a fresh start. Maybe cousin Bob would lend him the money. Well, anyway, he felt better about his options and needed to formulate a plan. When Bob brought him his food tomorrow, he would tell him about it. His despair was slowly turning into hope.

He left the truck and walked outside. The moon was full and giving off plenty of light. A few clouds drifted in front of the moon, throwing the farm into alternating shadows and light. He heard the sound of a horned owl in the distance. Just one more cigarette and he would go back to the truck to sleep.

As he was lighting up, he saw the headlights of a slow moving vehicle approaching the farm from the west. It turned into the driveway. Dwayne quickly went back into the barn and peered out a dusty broken window pane. It was a police car. He could feel the palms of his hands getting sweaty and clammy.

Two cops with flashlights got out of the car. He could see them talking and then walking toward the uninhabitable house that lay in ruins. He had been in the house several times and knew it well. It had a stuffy and stale smell about it an air of decay that hung like a shroud. The worst of the smells came from animal feces. The carpets were threadbare. Worn out and broken furniture was scattered about. The windows were uncovered and broken. There were scuff marks on the linoleum floors, and the wall paper had cigarette burns. Layers of dust and spider webs covered everything.

Once they went inside, he could follow their movements by the jerky movements of the flashlights. It was like watching fireflies through cracked and broken window glass. They explored the first floor and then went upstairs.

Dwayne panicked. He was sure they would go through the barn next. The smell of his own sweat nauseated him. His mind was racing and his mouth was dry. He felt goose bumps on his arms. His legs failed him and wouldn't move. He was so scared he was frozen to the earth. As he stared at the officers in the house, his eyes were wide open, and his breath was coming in hot hitching gulps. He had the frightening sensation that his life was in imminent danger, and he was powerless to defend himself.

Then instantly some unknown energy force overcame him and empowered him. He opened the barn doors and quickly ran to the truck. Sheer terror took over. He started the truck, raced out the barn, sped past the parked patrol car and turned west on County Road P. He jammed the accelerator to the floor and tightly gripped the steering wheel. He had no idea where he was going. The sensation of flight to somewhere safe totally consumed him. He was heading in the direction of home.

About a quarter of mile down the road at Richland Creek, a deer suddenly appeared from nowhere. The doe stopped in the middle of the road and stared into the headlights of his fast approaching vehicle. Dwayne immediately jumped on the brakes. They locked up. As the truck started sliding sideways, the unfolding tragic drama slowed down in front of his eyes. Time literally altered into slow motion. He felt the thud as the truck hit the deer, and he saw it flying across the hood. Then the truck careened off the road into a ditch, hit a small tree and rolled over. He was bloodied and knocked unconscious from the impact. When he came to, he was looking up at Captain Sigenthaler, who asked if he was okay. Before Dwayne could answer, he passed out.

CHAPTER 20

Jeff Fouts sat alone in his one bedroom apartment on 12th Avenue, drinking a cup of black coffee at his kitchen table. He had just finished breakfast, a bowl of cereal and a slice of whole wheat toast, while reading a copy of yesterday's Monroe Press. His eye brows were furrowed and he was thinking. It was seven thirty.

He was reading and scrutinizing the paper for the second time this morning. The bold print headlines on the front page reported that a suspect had been apprehended in connection with the Dr. Buckle murder. The article, written by Jake Neuberger, stated that the suspect, Dwayne Burkhalter, was currently in the hospital. The story highlighted the deer and truck accident on County Road P and a statement from Police Chief Johns. The statement from the chief was brief. He said that Burkhalter was a person of interest and the investigation was ongoing. It would be several days until Burkhalter was released from the hospital. At that time, they could possibility press charges. If that happened, he would then be remanded to the Green County Jail.

Fouts was a lawyer and a partner in the Newcomer, Pahnke and Fouts Law Firm, located a block off the square. He was forty-one years old and of average height. His striking blonde hair, green eyes and prominent chin made him easily recognizable around town. He was a starchy type of guy who was handsome and intelligent, but hard to warm up to. However, he could turn on the charm when needed. He was also separated from his wife, Diane, and their two children.

About six months ago, he got caught up in an affair with a client. A young woman named Joyce Shelton came to him for legal advice and counsel in a divorce proceeding against her cheating husband. She was divorcing her husband for adultery and mental cruelty. Joyce was twenty-six and worked as a hair dresser. She was a very attractive woman and a head turner when it came to men. Her long brunette hair, oversized breasts and short skirts got their attention. Some of the clothes she wore were so tight that they could easily be mistaken for a second skin. As she conferred with Fouts across his desk, she got his undivided attention. It wasn't her case that interested him. He immediately sized her up for his own sexual purposes. He reasoned that she was angry enough at her husband that she should be vulnerable to his compassion and comfort. He fanaticized about her between appointments.

It wasn't long before their scheduled appointments turned into flirting. She was seducing him with her beauty and sensuality. At one meeting, the top three buttons of her cotton blouse were undone exposing a lot of skin. It appeared to Fouts that her bra was made from black string. As she ran her hand up inside her blouse while talking, Fouts could hardly contain his urge to have her right in his office.

The tipping point came when she showed up for an appointment in a very short black skirt. As she sat facing Fouts, she crossed her legs in such a manner that she exposed herself. She was wearing red silk panties! Instantly and without warning, lust totally consumed him and he lost control. The siren call to raw passion was ringing in his head and body. He quickly jumped up from his desk and locked his office door. He made passionate love to her on the client's sofa in the office. She didn't resist. She made purring noises.

The ensuing affair took place in a cheap motel in Freeport, Illinois, about twenty miles south of Monroe. The secret blissful liaisons, the lying to his wife and all the rest energized him. Sneaking around like an adolescent made him feel young again. Joyce the goddess was his fantasy, and he obsessed on her. Her wild eyes and enthusiastic love making had him totally enthralled. The unrestrained passion was like nothing he had ever experienced before. He found himself bouncing and singing. Was this too good to be true?

Then it all came crashing down. Another lawyer in town told him that rumors were circulating about him. Apparently, Joyce was telling some of her friends about sleeping with a high profile lawyer and getting her legal fees for free. Fouts went nuts. He confronted her and she said it was true. She told him that the only reason she was screwing an old man like him was for the money she was saving. Besides, she had taken up with some guy her own age and was seeing them both at the same time. The instant humiliation sent him reeling to his knees. She laughed at him.

Having to tell his wife was devastating. The sad fact was that having two affairs had turned him into an excellent liar. After his first affair ended several years ago, Diane had forgiven him. He swore to her it wouldn't happen again. The emotional explosion this time would be intense when he told her about Joyce. He didn't have any options. The word was out and she would eventually hear it.

After his mea culpa, Diane went to pieces. He moved out of the house and into an apartment. He felt he owed it to her and the kids. A period of separation was needed. He rationalized that Diane, being of a strong Catholic faith, would be the answer to his problem. After his first affair, he discovered that divorce was out of the question for her and that saved his marriage. But, in the meantime, it was going to be pricey keeping up two places and he calculated that, after a while, she would ask him back for the sake of the children. During this interim, he had to figure out a way to get back into their lives.

Through Fout's eyes, this whole sordid affair was about him. He didn't give any credence to the emotional state of Diane and what she was experiencing. He couldn't appreciate Diane's feelings. To her, this infidelity was about trust, betrayal, lying and disloyalty. He learned from the first affair that Diane was so religious that she actually believed in her wedding vows. The church had taught her that a monogamous relationship was all about marriage, sex and childbearing. Divorce was a sin.

However, Fouts had a different world view of marriage. He told himself that it was okay to have sex outside of marriage. He was convinced of this and tried to explain to Diane that sex outside of marriage was actually good for their marriage. Diane wouldn't hear of it. As a practicing Catholic, she read the scriptures and prayed, and she had very conservative views, just like her parents. The other major point Fouts missed was that in a small town like Monroe infidelity and affairs mattered to the locals. Diane was acutely aware of this. In larger cities, people couldn't care less what their neighbors were doing, but not in Monroe. The social gossip could be unbearable. Fouts didn't seem to care. Diane did.

The flowers he sent to her were not working. Seeing the children was great, but they were confused and constantly asked him when he was coming home. It broke his heart when he had to leave them and return to the emptiness of his apartment. Diane had turned cold toward him. It seemed to him that the emotional gulf between them was widening. Was she growing apart from him? Was their marriage dying? This behavior wasn't in her nature, and it worried him. The separation was killing him. He missed the routine of family life. Even the women in his office were cool toward him. In spite of it all, he was confident that he could win her back. He would have to become a better actor.

He finished his coffee and went to his living room. He sat down in an overstuffed flowered chair, lit up a cigarette, and pondered. What was it that caused him to have an affair with Joyce?

In hindsight, he realized that she had the natural ability to sensually intoxicate men. In his experience as a lawyer, people from her class acted out from their emotions rather than their intellect. She could have easily been a hooker or worse. He should have immediately recognized this and left it alone. By contrast, Diane was educated, cute, faithful and a good mother. She was the perfect wife. So what was her reward for all her loyalty and nurturing? A cheating husband! The allure of easy sex and lust was his problem. Some men grow out of this and become good husbands and fathers. For Fouts, he couldn't bridge that gap. He felt like a fool, but he also knew in his heart of hearts there would probably be a next time.

As he stared out the window at the beginning of another sunny day, he reflected on a point in time after their second child was born. Diane had become depressed. She was hard to live with. A recent divorcee he knew through work started putting some subtle moves on him. The flirting was turning into lust, and he couldn't control himself. Something was terribly wrong and he knew it, but he couldn't keep his emotions in check. The guilt he felt wasn't enough to stop him. The woman wasn't even very good looking, but the thrill of easy sex overwhelmed him. Then she abruptly dumped him and moved on. She thanked him for being a bridge to another relationship.

While all this was going on, Diane was dealing with her depression. She also had a strong sense that something was wrong. Fouts was distant and had seemingly abandoned her. She pressed him relentlessly until he caved in and told her the truth. He pleaded for forgiveness and mercy. And it worked. Diane forgave him, partly because she felt it was her fault because of the depression, but she forgave him mostly for religious reasons.

Now he was in a jam. How could he reconcile with her after a second affair? The trust from their marriage was gone. He needed to do something that bordered on atonement. He needed to touch her faith somehow to win her back again.

After reading the paper this morning, he had an idea. That's why the article concerning the arrest of Burkhalter got his undivided attention. He was working out the start of a plan. The solution to his problem with Diane seemed suddenly clear, a moment of clarity. A smile crept across his face as he started to conjure up a strategy to get Diane back. His plan was simple enough on the surface. He would defend Burkhalter pro bono. It was brilliant! After all, it shouldn't be too difficult to argue the innocence of Dwayne Burkhalter.

CHAPTER 21

Julie Stryker was attending a parish council meeting at St. Michael's. It was nine p.m., and the meeting was starting to wrap up. She was sitting near the conference table in the church library where the folks were gathered. Father Bernard was at the head of the table, and the ten council members had their heads down following the agenda. Everyone seemed tired and was anxious for the meeting to end so they could go home. Julie was taking notes on upcoming parish events to get the dates, so she could adjust her schedule if necessary. She was planning a trip to Colorado to visit her family and didn't want to be gone too long. After all, she was the consummate church volunteer.

Suddenly the door to the library opened. Everyone turned and saw Diane Fouts standing there. She weakly smiled and waved a greeting to the group. They ignored her and went back to the business at hand. Diane quietly tiptoed up to Julie, handed her a note and left. As the parish board agonized over the lateness of the hour, they didn't seem to notice or care about the exchange of the note. Julie slowly opened the white piece of paper and read, "We need to talk!" She then folded the note and put it into her purse, unaware that Father Bernard was staring at her.

The meeting ended with a prayer from Father Bernard. After the usual chit-chat all the members made for the exit. Out in the hallway, Julie spotted Diane talking to one of the board members. As she approached, Diane grabbed her by the arm and led her into a small church office off the hallway. The office had a small oak table, a couple of chairs and overflowing book shelves. It was a catch-all storage place. Once inside, Diane closed the door.

Father Bernard saw this and instantly his curiosity peaked. He got excited. After everyone was gone, he silently went into the adjoining office and closed the door. There was enough street lighting coming through the window that he didn't need to turn the light on. He quietly cleared some books from the top of a desk. He then took his shoes off and climbed upon the desk in his stocking feet. He was still about six inches shy of the air duct that led into the adjoining room. He strategically placed three large books below the duct and stood on them. He then placed his ear against the duct. The voices from the adjoining room were amazingly clear. Standing on the books was a little awkward for him, but he was determined.

Diane sat down in one of the two chairs and immediately broke into tears. Julie retrieved some tissues from her purse and handed them to her. She sat quietly across from her as the tears streamed down her friend's face. After a few moments, Diane began to compose herself. The tears stopped.

"Sorry about that," she said. "I received a phone call from Detective Gates asking for an appointment to see me. It was very upsetting."

"What did she say?" Julie asked.

"Gates told me that my name came up during their investigation of Dr. Buckle's murder. She was told from someone they interviewed that Diane Fouts may have some information concerning the doctor and his death."

She stopped talking and stared at a picture hanging on the wall, of the Shepherd standing in a pasture with some sheep. Julie remained still and quiet.

"I needed to talk to you after the call!" Diane suddenly said.

Julie reached over and grabbed her hand. She gently squeezed it. Diane smiled and seemed to relax.

"As you know, I am trying to put this whole incident behind me, but I can't! I can't sleep at night. The kids are getting on my nerves. I know it isn't their fault that Jeff and I are separated, but they keep asking me why their daddy isn't living at home. Then the shame of being raped is unbearable. Sometimes I blame myself, and then sometimes I curse Buckle! How could that pig do that to me! I didn't deserve it!"

Father Bernard gasped and almost lost his balance! He couldn't believe his own ears.

Diane's eyes welled up again and droplets of tears trickled down her face and off her chin. Julie gave her more tissues. Julie sat silent. Then she stood up and gently pulled Diane up to her. As the two women embraced one another, Julie could feel Diane trembling. After a short while she relaxed, and Julie let her go. They sat down again.

"Thank you." Diane said. "I need your advice. You are the only person I can trust. I know how badly your husband treated you and how St. Michael's and your faith pulled you through."

"How can I help?" Julie softly asked.

Father Bernard was sweating. He felt guilty as he surreptitiously listened to a very personal and heart wrenching conversation. He couldn't believe what he was hearing. The anguish in Diane's voice was chilling. He could feel the warmth in his cheeks, and he was angry. The emotions he was feeling told him one thing, but he had to hold himself in check. His immediate thought was to leave his roost and charge into the adjacent office to offer assistance and council. But he couldn't do that. He wasn't supposed to be there. His behavior had taken him to a place where trust had been violated. Nevertheless, he couldn't tear himself away from the air duct. He was fixated on the drama taking place next door. He offered up a quick prayer for forgiveness and continued to listen as quietly as possible.

"I have only told you and Jeff about the rape. How do you think Detective Gates heard about it?" Diane said.

"Are you certain Gates knows about the rape? Did she mention it on the phone?"

"No she didn't. But I am convinced she knows!"

"Why?"

"Monroe gossip, I suppose. It is very hard to keep a secret here. It seems that everyone is related by blood, including first and second and third cousins, and the list goes on and on."

Julie nodded. She knew exactly what Diane was saying. A short pause followed and they both settled back into their chairs.

"I guess it really doesn't matter who told Gates," Diane said. "So, what do I tell Gates when she comes to the house?"

"Just tell her the truth." Julie replied.

"Should I tell her that I only told you and Jeff about the rape?"

"Yes. The police have a curious way of getting to the truth anyway."

"Do you think the rape will become public knowledge? You know, get into the newspaper?"

"I don't know. I wouldn't think so. The police are more interested in finding Dr. Buckle's killer. The rape will just be one more piece of background information for them. You don't know who killed Dr. Buckle, and they will be satisfied with that."

Diane looked relieved. She took a deep breath and silently reflected on what Julie just told her. She admired her friend. The common sense answers were comforting. The interview with Gates should be okay.

"Have you had any thoughts on who may have killed Dr. Buckle since our last conversation?" Julie asked.

Diane shook her head. "I have no idea," she softly said.

"How are things going with you and Jeff? Anything new on that front?" Julie asked.

Diane had to shift mental gears. She took a moment before she answered.

"Nothing has changed. I just don't trust him. As you know, my faith helped me to overcome his first affair. At the time I was depressed. When he told me about the adultery, I was reduced to rivers of tears and eating gallons of ice cream. I gained twenty pounds. The heartbreak was unbearable. The previous priest, Father Mark, told me that it was only a small hiccup in a marriage and that I should forgive him. There was a huge emphasis on the word forgiveness! That was when Jeff told me he was truly sorry and it would never happen again. I forgave him like the priest said and tried to put it out of my mind."

Father Bernard gasped again.

"Do you think you two will ever get back together?" Julie asked her.

"I don't know. How can I ever love a man I cannot trust? Constantly worrying and being suspicious of his every move would drive me insane. How can any marriage survive a partner who can't control his sexual desires? I have never refused his requests for sex. I just don't get it. How could he humiliate me a second time and totally ignore me as a loving wife and mother?"

The question hung in the air for some moments. Another tear appeared on her cheek. Neither woman spoke for several minutes.

"My mother was happy for me when I married Jeff. She gave me her blessing. I think Jeff being raised Catholic was all the assurance she needed."

"Did you need her blessing to marry him?"

"Yes, I suppose I did. When I started dating in high school, she told me to date only Catholic boys. She was very strict about this. In college I dated a Presbyterian guy who was very nice. He made me laugh. I didn't tell my mother. After about a month, I had to break it off. I was sure that she would find out."

Julie nodded. She fully understood what Diane was telling her.

"So tell me this. How do I get on with my life, living with an adulterous husband?"

Julie didn't say anything.

"After Jeff told me about his first affair, life for him went on like nothing happened. I was hurting inside and trying to recover from the emotional shock of it all. The humiliation of other people knowing was terrible. During this time he didn't offer me any support. The bit about forgiveness for an uncaring husband left a deep scar on my heart. I just had to learn to live with it. I tried to talk to him about my feelings, but he just clammed up. We never spoke about the affair again."

"I don't know how to answer your question," Julie said, "but I can offer this up. Maybe Jeff telling you about the affair and coming clean was a very selfish act on his part. It was a way to absolve himself of any guilt. In the process, he was hurting someone who didn't deserve to be hurt. You know, like the absolution the priest gives. Jeff must have felt that, since he confessed to you, that was all that was required. You obviously aren't a priest, but the same principle must have applied as far as he was concerned."

Diane caught her breath. "I never thought of it that way before."

"So what are you going to do?" Julie asked.

"When Detective Gates comes to visit, I will tell her the truth. Then I will have to work out a plan to leave Jeff. That will be messy, of course, but I can't trust him. I couldn't live through a third affair! Anyway, I think it will be worse on the kids if we stayed together. The tension between us wouldn't be healthy for them"

"So how about Father Bernard, do you plan to tell him?"

"No, I don't think so. I feel that I have used up all the forgiveness that God allotted me."

The two women got up and hugged once again.

"Thank you for seeing me. You are my best friend!" Diane said.

As they left the little room, Julie offered her good wishes and asked her to call her after the meeting with Gates. Diane said she would.

Once they had left the church, Father Bernard climbed down from his perch on the desk. He put his shoes on and locked the church building as he left. Once safely back in the rectory, he went directly to bed. He tossed and turned and couldn't sleep. Around four a.m. he decided that he needed to see Jeff Fouts. After that decision, he fell fast asleep.

CHAPTER 22

Sam sat behind her desk at the P.D. She was alone in the briefing room. The other officers had finished their updates for the day and left for their shifts. She was wearing a faded pair of blue jeans and a cream colored button-down cotton shirt. A new pair of penny loafers rounded out her casual dress for the day. A pair of sun glasses sat on her desk. A splash of scent left a sweet fragrance lingering in the room.

She had just finished some paperwork and put it in her out-basket. The ticking clock on the wall said seven thirty a.m. She was waiting for Drew. He said he would pick her up at eight. She had spoken to him twice after Janet's insistence. With Burkhalter in the hospital recovering from his injuries, the whole police department relaxed. In fact, the whole city breathed a sigh of relief. Chief Johns approved a couple of days off for both Sam and Sigenthaler after the long hours they had put in on the Dr. Buckle murder. That gave Sam the opportunity to spend some much needed quality time with Drew.

Sigenthaler was delighted, of course. He was convinced that Burkhalter was the killer, and once the gun was found, he would be tried for murder. He needed the time off to mend fences with his wife and family. Once again, he told Sam that he could never be a detective. The grinding pace of working long hours with next to no time off would ruin his marriage. He loved police work, but he wanted to work regular routine hours and have a family life. Sam understood.

Even Roger Nussbaum was thrilled with the capture of Burkhalter. He didn't spare the praise for Chief Johns and the P.D. for their quick and professional work in finding the killer. His comments made front page headlines in the Monroe Press. He had called Johns twice to make sure that he read all his quotes.

Sam was a little nervous as she waited for Drew. She realized that she had treated him badly. Her independent go-getter personality and focus had completely abandoned him since the day of the murder. She obsessed on the case, and it had totally consumed her. Nothing else mattered. She found herself so self-involved and so self-centered that she had ignored him and his feelings. When she took the time to think about it, she knew that her workaholic approach to her job wasn't healthy. But, at the same time, she didn't seem to know how to fix it.

Hearing Drew's voice on the phone was wonderful. She realized how much she missed him. His soothing voice relaxed her. He was very understanding and supportive of her. He suggested that they go to Galena, Illinois, for the day to get away from Monroe and just have some fun. She jumped at the chance. She told him to pack an overnight bag.

Galena, known for its history and historical architecture, was a popular tourist destination about sixty miles west of Monroe. At one time Galena was the hub on the Mississippi River between St. Louis, Missouri, and St. Paul, Minnesota. Former Civil War General and President Ulysses S. Grant had a residence there, as well as several other war generals. The natural beauty of the land, the city and the many downtown shops made it a quaint destination. Sam was really looking forward to spending the day with Drew.

Glancing at the clock again, she saw that Drew would be there in fifteen minutes. She only had one more piece of paper on her desk to put away. She turned it over a couple of times in her hand and then stared at it. On the paper were pencil-drawn circles with names printed inside of them. In the middle circle was the name Dr. Buckle. To the right of him was another circle with the name Dwayne Burkhalter. Below that circle was another one with the name Rita Steffes. Sam had drawn straight lines between the three circles forming a triangle.

To the left of Dr. Buckle was another circle with the name Diane Fouts. Sam had drawn a circle below her with a question mark inside it. It formed another triangle. And finally she had a circle with Ingrid Lindquist with a crossed-out line drawn through it. That circle was at the bottom of the paper and didn't connect with any of the other circles.

Looking at the circles on the paper reminded her of one her science classes where she drew atoms, protons and neutrons all spinning around one another. The circles helped her to organize her thoughts. When Dr. Buckle raped Rita, Dwayne was brought into the picture, the third point of that triangle. Ingrid Linguist mentioned Diane Fouts as a person of interest.

What could that mean? Was there a relationship between her and Dr. Buckle? Sam would have to suss it out. If she found something of significance then the third point to that triangle would come into play. Who would be the unknown person in the remaining empty circle? Sam reasoned that someone would turn up sooner or later to be in the circle with the question mark. Too many questions and not enough answers. She had crossed out Lindquist from her circle diagram. She was not a suspect in Sam's mind.

Sam jumped when the dispatcher called to her and said she had a visitor. She quickly put the paper away, grabbed the overnight bag beside her desk, and hurried to the front door of the police station. She saw Drew standing there and waved to him. He looked very handsome in blue jeans and a Wisconsin Badgers tee shirt. Drew waved back and gave her a big smile. Sam knew this was going to be a great get-a-way.

Drew gave Sam a big hug and tossed her overnight bag into the backseat of his red Ford Galaxie 500 convertible. Just as they were pulling out of the parking lot, Shirley, the dispatcher, suddenly ran out of the station and flagged them down. She said Sam had an urgent phone call. It was from Cal Thompson at the Silver Bay P.D. Sam immediately jumped out of the car and ran back into the station. Drew backed up the car and parked.

When Drew entered the station, he saw Sam sitting in a chair beside the dispatch table talking on the phone. He could see the tense muscles bulging in her hand as she tightly gripped the telephone receiver. She stared at the opposite wall not saying anything. Her face was ashen. It was as if she had seen a ghost.

Sam was unaware that Drew and the dispatcher were looking at her. Her heart was racing, and she felt numb. She was in shock. The phone call that she was hoping for over the years just came in. The call was so unexpected. She wasn't prepared for it. She felt overwhelmed. After the call, a raging flood of memories came screaming back and inundated her mind. At Mach speed, she was reliving the events surrounding her dad's death.

Then, suddenly, she snapped out of it. She slammed the phone back down on its cradle. Looking at Drew, she said she needed to go to Silver Bay at once. The P.D. had just found the stolen car that the killers were driving the night her Dad was killed!

"I need to go at once! This minute!" she exploded.

"I'll drive you," Drew hastily replied.

"You'd that for me?"

"Of course, I will!"

Drew grabbed a piece of paper from his blue jeans pocket and handed it to Shirley.

"Please call this number in Galena and cancel our hotel reservation for tonight."

Sam and Drew half-walked, half-ran to Drew's car and jumped in. He gunned the engine as he sped out of the parking lot. It took him only a couple of minutes to wind his way out of Monroe onto Wisconsin Highway 11 heading east to Silver Bay.

Sam sat in silence, staring at the road as Drew sped along at ten miles over the speed limit. He glanced at her a couple of times as the scenery flew past. The wind was whipping at her hair. Drew didn't say anything. He realized that Sam was mentally processing this new information and needed her space. Her eyebrows were pinched, and her eyes were focused straight ahead as if watching a movie. For the next hour and a half, not a word passed between them. As they enter the city limits of Silver Bay, Sam directed him to the P.D.

When he pulled into the parking lot of the Silver Bay P.D., an elderly gentleman in a police uniform exited the building and greeted them. Sam got out of the car and hugged him. She introduced Drew to Police Chief Cal Thompson. They immediately got into a black and white police car. Sam climbed into the front seat, and Drew settled into the back seat. As Thompson drove, he filled them in.

"Some newly elected government officials decided that a highway beautification program was needed. The funding was secured to start cleaning up rural roads. On Highway 83 between Paddock Lake and Salem, the work was going well until the cleanup crews came across an abandoned car in a ditch. The steep embankment had kept the car hidden from view for years. The crew called in the license plate number, and the car turned out to be the very one the killers stole the night your dad was murdered."

Sam was listening intently. She nodded.

"The car is in tough shape. We called a tow truck service to deliver it to an impound area so we could go over it. I don't hold out much hope to find anything useful. Not after all these years. But I told the towing service not to remove the car until we arrived. I wanted you to see it as we found it."

"Thank you," Sam whispered.

As they pulled up behind the tow truck, Sam jumped out of the patrol car, went to the edge of the embankment and peered over it. She just stared at the car. Thompson and Drew soon joined her. She slid down the embankment on her butt and examined the rusty driver's side door. Drew could readily see years of dirt and decay on the car. Leaves and twigs and broken branches had half buried it. He also saw the weeds that surrounded the car, the spiny thistle, the creeping jenny, the Dame's violet and poison ivy. He called down to Sam to watch out for the poison ivy. She ignored him as she circled the car.

When Sam had climbed back up the embankment, Thompson nodded to the tow truck driver. Then they drove back to the P.D. Thompson said if they found anything interesting after examining the car he would call. He reassured Sam that the case was still open and not to give up hope. She thanked him. Thompson suggested they all get something to eat, but Sam politely refused. She hugged him and got back into Drew's car. After shaking hands with Thompson, Drew jumped back into his car and started engine. He headed back to the highway that would take them to Monroe.

Suddenly, Sam told him to take a right at the next intersection and directed him to the cemetery where Earl was buried. It was located on the north edge of Silver Bay's city limits. Drew was surprised to see the poor condition of the cemetery. The overgrown grass, weeds and leaning tombstones were depressing. The grounds had the appearance of being unmaintained and forgotten. Some of the grave markers were turned over, and empty beer cans were scattered about. Sam guided Drew along the broken and bumpy asphalt pavement to a place near the back of the cemetery. He stopped the car and she got out. She walked the short distance to a familiar grave marker and fell to her knees. Drew silently followed her, looking at the overgrown trees and shrubs. This was not a cemetery that he felt comfortable in. He felt uneasy, as if it was haunted or something.

"Hi, Dad," she said. "It's me—Sam. You won't believe this, but after all these years we found the missing car." She paused.

"You know, I never gave up hope in finding it. Cal Thompson will be going over it for fingerprints and anything else he can find to identify your killers. I promised you that we would find them and bring them to justice. Now finding the car is an omen. It's a start. It was as if God was telling me not to give up."

Sam stopped talking and wiped the tears from her eyes. She rocked back on her heels. Drew stood behind her, totally awe struck by the poignant moment. The outpouring of raw emotion from Sam was heartbreaking. Her voice shook as she spoke. It was the first time in his life that he witnessed such a pure and true expression of love. He was overcome by the emotional outpouring for one of life's tragedies. Then Sam suddenly spoke again.

"The guy behind me is Drew Nelson. He is really a nice guy. I think you would have liked him."

Drew gasped, but Sam didn't seem to notice and kept talking to her father.

"I will be back to see you again after we have found the killers. It shouldn't be too long now. I love you, Dad. I love you."

After a few moments, Sam got back to her feet. She bowed her head and said a silent prayer. On the way back to the car, she told Drew that one day she was moving Earl to the Green Lawn Cemetery in Monroe.

As they journeyed back to Monroe, Drew asked her how she was feeling. He could see that her shoulders were relaxed as she slumped back into the car seat.

"I feel a little confused," she said after a few moments. "I have been waiting so long for the car to be found. I always thought that once we had it that would lead us directly to the killers. But now I'm not so sure. Finding the car brought back many sad memories. Seeing it in such a state of disrepair and decay reminded me how many years had gone by."

She stopped talking, but Drew remained quiet.

"The realization that we may never find the killers is horrifying. I promised Dad that someday I would bring them to justice, and now I feel that I am letting him down."

She was speaking in a very tired and monotone voice. "If we ever find the killers after all this time, it will probably be by sheer luck."

"I think you will find them," Drew said. "Life has a way of balancing things out."

Sam closed her eyes and laid her head back on the seat. The breeze felt good on her face. The miles melted away under the car tires as they headed west.

"How is your mom doing?" Drew asked.

Sam opened her eyes. "She's doing okay. She has really adapted well to the nursing home and enjoys her new friends there. Many wonderful people work with her. I think she is very happy, and, for that, I am glad."

"How about you; are you happy?"

The question just hung in the air. Drew reached over and took her hand in his. She didn't resist.

"No," she finally said. "If I am honest with myself, I am not happy." She paused a moment as the car cruised along. "My life is passing me by. I have morphed into my job. I love being a detective. The challenge of it and the excitement of it all is my passion. When I get involved in a case, all my other problems go away. It is hard to explain how energized I get. And once I catch the bad guy, it's like Christmas and the Fourth of July all wrapped up into one package."

"Do you think that's healthy? I mean, are you happy just grinding it out?" Drew asked.

"Happy isn't the right word. Obsession is probably closer to the way I feel, and no, I don't think it's healthy."

"What would make you happy then?"

Without hesitation Sam exclaimed, "To catch my dad's killer!"

"After you do that, then what?" Drew asked.

Sam didn't have an answer. In fact, she had never really thought about it.

She slid over on the bench seat and leaned against him. Drew put his arm around her. She snuggled even closer. Her left hand rested on his right leg. Then she laid her head on his shoulder and closed her eyes. She was exhausted and fell asleep. Drew listened to the sounds of her slow rhythmic breathing. She was fast asleep. They would be in Monroe in thirty minutes.

Drew pulled up to the curb in front of Sam's apartment. When he turned the car off, Sam stirred and woke up. It was dark. She immediately invited him up to get something to eat. She was famished. He retrieved the overnight bags, put the cover up over his car and locked it. As they walked up the sidewalk, Sam grabbed his arm and squeezed it. She knew she was going to get a good night's sleep. She had known a lot of self-centered men with big egos, but Drew was different. His ego didn't trump his humility. She loved him for that.

The following morning Sam was up early and showered before Drew woke up. She was excited. Having Drew in her bed was fantastic. Her plan for the morning was to see Sharon at the nursing home. She would introduce her to Drew and fill her in on the car being found after all these years. Sam was convinced that Sharon would be delighted with the news. They had both suffered enormously after Earl's murder and closure is what they needed. This was another step in the process. Drew was agreeable to the visit and enjoyed the hearty breakfast Sam prepared for him. He commented on her excitement. She was pumped up!

After arriving at the nursing home, they found Sharon in the day room.

Sam immediately spotted her chatting with two other women, her back turned to them. She touched her on the shoulder. Sharon turned around and smiled. She introduced Sam to the other ladies, and Sam then introduced Drew to the group as a good friend. Sharon looked at him and then to Sam and smirked. So they are only good friends? Indeed!

The other women excused themselves, and Sam and Drew sat down in the vacated chairs.

"I have some good news," Sam began. "The car that the killers used the night dad was murdered has been found! After all these years, we finally have a break in the case!"

Sharon stared impassively at her. Sam was taken aback. She had expected something more from her mom; she got only silence.

"Did you understand what I just said?"

Sharon seemed lost in thought. She looked at Drew and back to Sam.

"Yes, Samantha, I heard you," she began just above a whisper. "I have suffered all these years after his death, but now I am happy. Moving to Monroe saved my life. I loved your father very much, but you always told me I needed to get on with my life. I have wonderful friends here. This may seem like a cruel thing to say, but not thinking about Earl and his horrific death has made my life better."

Sam couldn't believe what she was hearing. "But I thought you wanted his killers caught and brought to justice. I have dedicated my life to finding them!"

"Yes, I do. And that would be a great thing. But I need to live my life, too. I have found happiness here, and I don't want to dwell in the past. Can't you understand that?"

Actually, Sam didn't understand that. She had always assumed that finding Earl's killers would bring happiness and peace into her mom's life. Hearing her mother say these words puzzled her. Had she been wrong in her assumptions? The next thought that popped into her mind scared her. If Sharon had moved on with her life, what about herself? Was she so stuck in the past that now she was the only prisoner left of their fate? Had her mom escaped? When Drew asked her what would make her happy was her answer an honest one?

Drew sat passively listening to Sam and her mom sort out these difficult disclosures of their intimate feelings. It seemed pretty clear to him that Sharon had left the past behind and was healing. She didn't want to hear about the car. She didn't want to go back.

He could also see that Sam was struggling with this new truth. As Sam sat quietly staring at the table and thinking, Sharon caught his eye and smiled. He smiled back. In the silence, he instinctively liked Sharon. She was a woman who had gone to hell and back and survived.

Wherever Sam's thoughts had taken her, she was back. She stood up and announced that they needed to leave. She went to Sharon, leaned over and hugged her. Drew shook her hand and said how happy he was to meet her. Sharon smiled and said that next time they came they could have a longer visit. With that, Sam headed for the exit, carrying a heavy burden in her heart. How could she have been so wrong?

CHAPTER 23

Jeff Fouts slowed his pace as he turned the corner on 10th Street and stopped to admire the square. The sun was radiantly shining on the courthouse, making it glow. The majestic Romanesque-style courthouse located in the center of Monroe's historic square was the county seat. Its beautiful architecture was accented by arched porticos and polished marble pillars. High windows emphasized the distinct quality of the white granite block. Chiming bells in the soaring clock tower above the courthouse announced the time of day and gave the place old world charm.

Inside the courthouse, the lawyer walked up a flight of marble steps to the top floor and entered the court chambers. He walked across the highly polished wood floors to his defense table facing the bench of Green County Judge Myron Dietmeire. He was early; he wanted to be there before Burkhalter arrived. Dwayne Burkhalter was being escorted into the courthouse by Sheriff's deputies in a wheel chair.

Glancing at the south end of the room, Fouts could see the gallery chairs filling up. The case had received a lot of attention, and curious onlookers were packing themselves in. Everyone in Monroe seemed to know everyone else, and Dwayne Burkhalter was no exception. There were hushed whispers as they waited. It was a standing-room-only crowd, and this was just a preliminary hearing to bind Burkhalter over for trial. The Burkhalter family sat in the front row. Mrs. Burkhalter was wiping salty tears from her face. The rest of the family sat stone-faced, looking straight ahead.

Fouts spotted Jake Neuberger from the Monroe Press, chatting with some locals. He knew his interview quotes would make the front page headlines after the hearing.

Two oversized murals painted by the German artist, Franz Rohrbeck, hung in the courtroom, one behind the judge's bench and the other on the opposite wall. Framed pictures of all the Green County Judges, past and present, hung in a row on the west wall.

A murmur went up from the crowd as the D.A. arrived. He nodded to Fouts as he made his way to his desk. He opened his brief case and laid out several papers in front of him. The hearing was scheduled for ten thirty a.m.

Then suddenly a gasp went up as Burkhalter was wheeled into court. He looked terrible. His head was bandaged with white cotton gauze, and his jaw was wired shut. He was discolored, black and blue, from the accident. He looked very thin. Dwayne stared straight ahead with no expression on his face as the deputies parked him next to Fouts' desk. Fouts reached over and squeezed his arm and smiled. Then he leaned over and whispered to him. The onlookers became very quiet with all eyes glued on Dwayne.

A few moments later, Judge Dietmeier entered the court room dressed in his judicial robes. Everyone stood, except Dwayne. Dietmeier gaveled the court into session and nodded to the court clerk.

Burkhalter wasn't listening to the proceedings. As the judge, the D.A. and Fouts bantered back and forth, he slowly turned his head to look at the gallery. They were all looking at him. He saw his parents and siblings in the front row. As he scanned the standing-room-only crowd, he couldn't find Rita. The only one from the Brass Tap he saw was Bonnie. When they made eye contact, she smiled at him. So much for bar friends.

As he sat staring at the mural above Judge Dietmeier's head, Dwayne felt confused. He was convinced that he should not be convicted of killing Dr. Buckle. But one never knows for certain. The very thought of being found guilty made his stomach hurt. In general, he didn't trust lawyers. A friend of his was overcharged by a lawyer once and didn't have any choice but to the pay the overage. The feeling among Dwayne's friends was that the common man had no power when dealing with lawyers. So when Jeff Fouts visited him in hospital and told him that he was going to defend him for free, Dwayne clammed up. He immediately thought that the Country Club lawyers were getting together to screw him, and since Dr. Buckle was a member of the club, they were looking for a sacrificial goat to pin the murder on.

Fouts had visited Dwayne in the hospital the previous evening. The doctor had given the okay for Dwayne to be released to appear in court, and Fouts told him the hearing today was only to set a trial date. He also told him that the D.A.'s case was entirely circumstantial. He was basing his case on the fact that Dwayne owned a hand gun and he had no alibi for the night of the murder, thanks to Rita. Also, he was going to prove that Dwayne had a temper and was avenging the rape of his girlfriend. The police had convinced the D.A. that once they found the gun they could convict.

Fouts and the D.A. had worked out a deal in which Dwayne would be remanded to his parents until the trial. This meant he wouldn't have to wait in jail for the trail to begin, and his parents could nurse him back to good health. No one considered him a flight risk.

During the dissemination of all this information, Dwayne lay silently in his hospital bed looking at the ceiling. He didn't trust Fouts. In Dwayne's mind, Fouts and his buddies had gotten together at the Country Club and discussed his guilt and laid out a game plan to convict him. The Bastards!

Fouts asked him where the gun was hidden. The bullets that killed the doctor were fired from a Smith and Wesson .38 caliber handgun. If they had Dwayne's gun, they could prove the bullets weren't fired from his gun, and he would go free. Bull Shit! How did he know my gun was a .38?, Dwayne thought.

Dwayne had purchased the gun from some guy he didn't know at the Brass Tap. It was closing time, and the stranger had run up a sizable bar tab and needed the money. Several of the patrons turned the gun sale down, but Dwayne bought it to impress Rita. He kept it in the glove box of his pickup truck until the night he pulled it out to threaten Dr. Buckle. When he was hiding from the police, he threw the gun down the abandoned well shaft on the old farm property. No way was he going to give this information to Fouts. He was convinced the gun was going to be used against him. That's the way the system works. He was no fool! He had heard about all the deals made at the Country Club.

Fouts got very angry at him when he wouldn't tell him where the gun was hidden. Since Dwayne couldn't talk because his jaw was wired shut, Fouts kept handing him pieces of paper to write down his answers. The paper remained blank.

Eventually Fouts lost his temper and yelled at him, "You stupid, stupid, stupid kid! I can save your life, and you don't care!" Fouts said he was going to talk to Dwayne's parents after the hearing. Hopefully, they could reach him and get the gravity of the situation into his pea-size brain. His life was on the line, and he needed to fully appreciate that and to cooperate. He needed to trust him. Jeff Fouts told him that he was his savior!

Dwayne felt the pressure of a hand on his arm. He looked over; Fouts was looking at him. Fouts stood up and explained to the judge that, since his client couldn't talk, he was entering a plea of not guilty for him. Judge Dietmeier ordered that Burkhalter would be bound over for trial. In the meantime, he would be remanded to his parents. The D.A. had no objections. The judge then graveled the proceedings closed and left the courtroom.

The crowd immediately stood up and started buzzing about the proceedings. Jake Neuberger made a beeline to Fouts and ushered him to the side of the courtroom for the interview. Dwayne's family made their way through the noisy crowd to wheel him out. Bonnie was with them. As they struggled to remove Dwayne from the crowded courtroom, Bonnie squeezed through the throng and touched Dwayne's arm. He turned and looked at her. She saw fear in his eyes. She gently held onto his arm and whispered to him that everything was going to be okay. Dwayne looked away.

CHAPTER 24

Father Bernard was drinking a cup of coffee, staring out the window of his office at St. Michael's. The fresh Danish on his desk was being ignored. It had taken him two tries to get an appointment with Jeff Fouts. They agreed to meet in his law office at one thirty. The priest decided to walk the short distance to the law office just off the square on 10th Street. He was a little nervous about the meeting. He told Fouts that he had some concerns and was very vague about the reason for the meeting. Fouts seemed annoyed at the request at first, but agreed to meet anyway. He told the priest he had only thirty minutes.

As he sipped his coffee, Father Bernard reviewed the facts as he understood them. Jeff and Diane Fouts had been married for several years and had two children. Diane and the kids were regular attendees at the church. Jeff never darkened the door except for Easter and Christmas Mass. And then it was probably under duress.

When they separated the first time, Diane was humiliated. The whole city of Monroe seemed to know what had happened. The affair was ripe for tongue wagging gossip since it involved a high profile attorney. Diane sought counseling from another priest. The priest was unable to get them to sit down together, so he advised Diane to forgive him to save the marriage. From what he heard through the air duct, he would have handled the situation differently.

Now that a second affair had occurred and they were once again separated, he needed to take action. He didn't want to make the same mistake as Father Mark. If he could talk to Jeff and make him see how damaging his behavior was to Diane and the children, then repentance could be achieved. He knew in his heart that he had to do a better job than his predecessor.

The one problem that bothered him was the rape. He was agonizing over it. He could understand why Diane didn't report it. But after telling her husband, why hadn't he done something? After all, he was an attorney. He would know perfectly well the legal avenues to follow to pursue charges against Dr. Buckle. Why didn't he do anything? Diane was obvious in pain, and if Jeff truly loved her . . . . He couldn't finish his thought.

He glanced at the clock on his desk, and it was time to leave. He told the church secretary that he was going out on a call and would be back in an hour. She didn't ask where he was going.

The day was sunny and pleasant, and his walk to the square was uninterrupted. He waved at two cars honking their horns as they passed him along 20th Avenue. He recognized the parishioners in both cars. Before he knew it, he was there. The sign in the window announced the Law Offices of Newcomer, Pahnke and Fouts. As he reached for the door knob, he hesitated. He suddenly broke into a sweat. Was he having second thoughts? If the truth be told, he hardly knew Jeff Fouts. Maybe he should have mentally rehearsed his meeting better. It seemed pretty easy thinking about it at the church, but now, standing there in the street, he wasn't so sure. He lifted up a short prayer and entered the office.

The law office was home to three attorneys. It had a very nice foyer and adjoining waiting area. The faint aroma of vanilla from a lit candle greeted visitors. Oriental throw rugs covered the polished hardwood floors. A few outdoor Wisconsin nature paintings and a team picture of the Green Bay Packers signed by Coach Vince Lombardi were hung on the walls. The receptionist was sitting at an oak table, with filing cabinets lined up like soldiers behind her. A hallway along the west wall led to the attorney's offices.

When Father Bernard went up to the receptionist table, he was surprised. He was greeted by Dorothy Ackerman. He had totally forgotten that she worked there. Dorothy was a dedicated church volunteer. After her husband died at age fifty, she was able to get a job as the receptionist at the firm.

She smiled at him. "Hello Father. What brings you here today?"

"I am here to see Jeff Fouts," he replied. "I have a one thirty appointment."

Dorothy checked the appointment calendar on her desk and smiled. "Why, yes, you do. I must have missed it this morning. Mr. Fouts is in with a client right now, but he should almost be finished. Please have a seat. Can I get you a cup of coffee?" Father Bernard declined and sat in a soft cushioned chair next to the window. He watched as Dorothy sorted some papers and took them to a filing cabinet.

About five minutes later, Jeff Fouts appeared with a client, a middle-aged man wearing spectacles and sporting a moustache. Father Bernard didn't recognize him. Not from Monroe. The two of them had a brief conversation in the foyer and the man left. Fouts then turned to Father Bernard, and they shook hands and exchanged greetings. Father Bernard followed him back to his office.

Fouts motioned for him to sit in a very comfortable high-backed leather chair in front of his desk. Dorothy suddenly appeared at the door as if on command. Fouts offered the priest a cup of coffee, which he refused. Then Fouts waved Dorothy off, and she left them.

While Fouts was seating himself behind his desk, Father Bernard noticed a framed picture of the family sitting on his desk. The picture must have been taken out west somewhere, because they were all dressed up in Western attire. The rest of the office had framed college and law diplomas hanging on the walls. An ornate banjo-style pendulum clock hung on the wall to the left of Fouts' desk. A couple of oak bookcases, stuffed with law books, lined the walls. Since the office was located in the interior of the building, it had no outside window. The office had the appearance and feeling of being in a well-lit cave.

Fouts leaned forward in his chair and put his elbows on his desk. As he stared at the priest, he clasped his hands together and made a steeple with his index fingers. He didn't say anything.

Father Bernard could feel cold sweat running from his armpits down his arm. He was very uncomfortable. In fact, he felt intimidated.

"The reason I made the appointment to see you today is that I am concerned about your family," he began.

Without hesitation or showing any emotion, Fouts asked, "Did my wife send you?"

"Oh, no, she didn't." Father Bernard quickly responded.

"Then why are you here?"

Father Bernard immediately sensed this was a mistake. Fouts was making his visit very painful for him. The only option he had was to plow ahead and say his piece.

"Look," he began, "Diane and the children are a vital part of our church family at St. Michael's. Everyone there loves and adores them. I wanted you to know that I am available to help. It is apparent to all of us that Diane is experiencing some level of discomfort and emotional pain."

After he said that, Father Bernard slumped back down into his chair and waited.

"What do you know about our marriage?"

Father Bernard gasped. He didn't expect the question.

"I know that you and Diane were separated a few years ago over an affair you had. I know that she forgave you and you got back together. I know that recently you had a second affair, and you are separated again."

Fouts didn't say anything. His eyes narrowed. He just glared at the priest.

"Is that all you know?"

"Well, there is something else."

Father Bernard hesitated. Should he bring up the rape? He always felt that honesty was the best policy. If everything was out in the open, then the healing process could begin. He steeled himself as Fouts' eyes were now narrowly focused on him like a laser. Somehow his eyes looked evil.

"I know about the rape," he whispered.

Fouts immediately sat back in his chair, then returned to the edge of his chair again. It was like he took a body blow in a fight. His steeple fingers became a fist. He swiveled ninety degrees in his chair and stared at the wall with his diplomas. His eyes glazed over. He instantly became lost in thought and oblivious to the presence of the priest.

Fouts reviewed in his mind how he had been trying to get back with his wife. She was being stubborn and said she needed her space. He could understand how the second affair had devastated her.

On the afternoon of the rape, Diane told him that she had dropped the kids off at a friend's house. She was working the second shift at the hospital, so the timing worked out perfectly. The Smith family owned a vacation home in northern Wisconsin and insisted that Diane's kids join their kids for the weekend. Lots of swimming, boating, water skiing, fishing and bon fires were planned. Everyone was ecstatic about the trip. Jeff thought the plan was a great idea, because, with the kids away, he hoped to get in some quality time with Diane.

The following day he tried to call her, but the phone went unanswered. Around three p.m. he called the hospital to talk to her. He was told that she had called in sick. He tried the house again, but still no answer. After work he stopped by the Blumen Keuner Shoppe on the square and bought an expensive bouquet of flowers from Mrs. Brown. He went back to his apartment, showered and ate a quick supper of leftovers. With flowers in hand, he rang the doorbell of his house at seven p.m.

After a few minutes, he saw Diane peek out through the curtains hanging next to the front door. She slowly opened the door, and Fouts stepped in. She was dressed only in a light blue cotton bathrobe. Her hair was wet, as though she had just emerged from a shower. Her bare feet sunk into the carpet. She just stood there staring at him. She looked as if she were in shock.

"What's the matter?" he asked. "I heard you were sick."

Diane suddenly broke into tears and raced up a flight of carpeted stairs to their bedroom. Fouts laid the flowers on a table in the foyer and followed her. Once in the bedroom, he saw her standing by an open window weeping. She was looking down into the backyard.

"For God's sake, Diane, tell me what's wrong!"

Diane slowly walked over to him, ripped open her bath robe and threw it on the bed. She was totally naked. Fouts immediately saw the bruising around her neck and arms.

He freaked out. "What the hell," he stammered. He reached out to touch her, but she drew away. "Tell me what happened to you, Diane!"

The sudden change in his demeanor seemed to awaken her. As they stood facing each other, she seemed to come to her senses. She told him how Dr. Buckle had forced her into a linen closet at the hospital and raped her. After he was done with her, he apologized and gave her some money. She threw the money back at him and fled.

Fouts was dumbstruck. He couldn't believe what he was hearing. He just stood there in disbelief with his mouth open. Dr. Buckle? It didn't make any sense.

"Did you report the assault to anyone?"

"No!"

"Why not?!"

Diane jumped at the loudness of his voice. "A world class surgeon raping a woman in hospital, nobody would believe me. Besides, it's just too embarrassing. I couldn't live with the humiliation of it, if the rape was made public." She sat down on the bed and starting sobbing again.

The anger Fouts felt was becoming unbearable. His face was deep red, and his fists ached as he tightly clenched them. "What do you want me to do?"

Diane brushed away the tears on her cheek with the back of her hand.

"You have already screwed up my life enough. I don't want you to do anything. I want you to leave me alone!"

Her words stabbed him in the heart. He felt humiliated and helpless. As she sobbed, he saw the gentle rising and falling of her breasts. The sight of her naked body excited him. The thought of someone else violating her body was maddening. She was the mother of his children and his faithful wife. He suddenly felt an overwhelming urge for revenge! He slammed his fist into the palm of his hand.

"That bastard will pay!" he screamed, and quickly left the bedroom. Somehow, he intuitively knew his fate was sealed as he raced down the staircase to his awaiting car.

Suddenly, Fouts became aware of his office surroundings and the priest. He swiveled his chair back to Father Bernard who had been patiently waiting during the prolonged silence.

"Thank you for coming today, Father," he abruptly said, "and I will call you if I need your help."

That said, he stood up and showed the priest to the front door, ushering him out of the building. Dorothy watched all this with a puzzled look on her face. Fouts shook his hand and immediately returned to his office.

As Father Bernard stood on the sidewalk, he was totally confused. Why was he dismissed so abruptly? Where did Fouts mentally go during that long silence?

The priest wasn't in the mood to go back to the church, so he headed west along 10th Street. He knew where he was going when he passed the First National Bank, Bahr's Variety Store and the Montgomery Ward store. At the end of the block, he tuned south and passed the Swiss Colony Store and came to a stop in front of Baumgartner's Cheese Store and Tavern. As he entered the store, a friendly voice rang out. Dave Goecks waved to him and motioned for him to join a small group of friends at his table. Father Bernard smiled. He immediately knew that this was going to be a cheap afternoon for him.

"Say, Father, did you know that it was against state law to serve a piece of apple pie in a public restaurant without a slice of cheese?" They all laughed heartily, and another round of beers was ordered.

CHAPTER 25

Chief Johns arrived back at his office at one thirty p.m. He was pleased. In just four short weeks since the murder, they had a suspect. Since Dwayne Burkhalter was charged, Johns had received a certain level of notoriety. Today for instance, Roger Nussbaum took him to lunch at the Ratskeller in the cellar of Turner Hall on 17th Avenue. The building was unique to Monroe, looking like a Swiss Chalet. Some of Nussbaum's pals were visiting from Madison, so he had invited the chief to join them.

The menu card was delightful. The chief surveyed the choices that had his mouth watering. The Bratwurst Platter was served with sauerkraut and Swiss green beans. The Wiener schnitzel was served with Swiss green beans. The Baked Cheese Pie was served with fresh fruit. He decided on the Cheese Pie, fresh fruit and a tossed salad. Since Nussbaum was paying, he ordered one beer and then another. All of Nussbaum's friends were ordering mixed drinks. To finish off his feast, he ordered a slice of Black Forest Chocolate cake and a cup of black coffee.

After they all ordered and the waitress hurried away, he sat back in his chair and looked around. Soft Swiss music added to the relaxing ambiance of the dining room. All the tables were covered with red-checkered tablecloths. The pictures on the walls highlighted a historical trip back in time featuring decades of Swiss culture. The waitresses were dressed in colorful Swiss dirndl dresses and white eyelet aprons, and they nodded to him as they passed his table, waiting on other customers.

The conversation around the table was all about Madison politics. Johns had no interest or opinions, so he remained quiet during all the back and forth banter. His interest was in the structure and routine of police work, where politics didn't enter in much when enforcing the law. The only exception, of course, was when the politicians weighed in if they felt they could garner more votes. Nussbaum was his obvious example.

After lunch Johns was stuffed and needed a nap. The hearty and generous portions added immense pressure to his waistline. He would have to loosen his belt buckle two notches. He appreciated the fact that the meal was free, but he would pay a heavy price in the afternoon. Maybe he should have passed on the invitation, but he didn't want to cross Nussbaum.

Johns had received several letters of congratulations from his police colleagues and well-wishers. It was embarrassing. What if Burkhalter wasn't the killer? How embarrassing would that be? The whole city was resting easier now that a suspected murderer was in custody and charged. Everyone seemed to be in a better mood. Even the chief was in a better mood with the diminished pressure from Nussbaum to find a suspect. However, the chief still had his doubts.

Captain Sigenthaler was leading the charge to get the evidence needed to try Burkhalter. He and Green County Sheriff's Deputy Pete Swenson were spending their days at the old farm in Clarno looking for the gun that killed Dr. Buckle. Sigenthaler boasted to his fellow officers that the gun would be found there. It was just a matter of time. The only complaint Johns received was from the Green County Sheriff about the overtime.

Detective Gates, on the other hand, wasn't so sure Burkhalter was the killer. She didn't think he had the smarts or the guts to carry out a premeditated murder. She didn't trust Rita and her version of the facts. The defense council seemed pretty cocky about proving Dwayne was with her at the time of the murder. Why was that? Could they prove it in court?

Sam had scheduled a meeting with Diane Fouts at her home. Ever since Ingrid Lindquist had mentioned hearing hospital gossip about this woman, Sam believed that Diane could shed some light on the investigation. Maybe Diane had some information that she didn't know she possessed. Sam felt a one-on-one with her was better than bringing Sigenthaler along. Besides, he seemed to like playing in the dirt with his friends at the farm.

As Johns stood in the doorway to his office, he surveyed the chaos on his desk and floor and shrugged his shoulders. According to Shirley, Jerome Pagel had a summer cold and had missed a couple days of work. Johns was anticipating that his summer intern would get him caught up on the mountains of paper on his desk, but now that seemed impossible. The only hope he had was for some kind of the end-of-the-world catastrophe, like, the police department burning down!

He eventually found his mail in a separate stack on his desk and gathered it all up in his arms. He went to the day room and located an empty desk along the east wall. He dumped the mail there and watched it scatter. Then he went to see Shirley. She had two more small piles of mail and a brown envelope from the Forensics Lab in Madison on her desk. The brown envelope was placed next to her telephone. Johns almost missed it.

Back in the day room, Johns seated himself behind the messy desk he had just created. He started sorting the mail by sender. Then he moved about two-thirds of the mail to a corner of the desk. He wrote Jerome's name in big letters on an envelope and placed it squarely in the middle of the new pile. Jerome could deal with that pile when he got back.

Lunch was getting the better of him, so Johns adjourned and made his way down the hallway to the restroom.

When he returned, Shirley came in to offer him a cup of steaming coffee. She had just put on a fresh pot. He welcomed the interruption and accepted the offer as Shirley looked over the mess.

"I would say you are about two weeks behind," she said.

"Remind me again what we're paying Jerome to do?"

Shirley laughed as she left, returning a few moments later with a streaming mug. Johns thanked her for the coffee as she returned to her desk.

Sipping his coffee, Johns picked up the brown envelope from the Forensics Lab. He couldn't remember sending anything analytical to the lab. This was probably just a backlog item he had forgotten about.

Johns cut the top off with a pair of scissors, and as he held the envelope upside down, a clear evidence bag containing two bullets fell out.

"What the hell?"

Johns reached inside the envelope and found a copy of a standard ballistics request form signed by him. He also found a report on the bullets and quickly scanned through the summary findings. In short, it read that both the bullets sent to the lab from the Monroe Police Department were fired from the same weapon, a Smith and Wesson .38-caliber handgun.

His mouth dropped open. He didn't immediately understand what he was looking at. What two bullets? He re-read the report again. He had a puzzled look on his face. Am I missing something here? he thought.

He called out to Shirley. Maybe she could shed some light on this mystery.

As she approached him, she had a strange look on her face. Standing in front of him looking at the evidence bag in his hand, she felt embarrassed.

She shifted nervously from foot to foot. She started to sweat a little. She felt as if she had betrayed the chief's confidence by going along with Jerome's little scheme. Johns instantly noticed her discomfort.

"I told Jerome not to do it," she began.

"Not to do what?"

"Jerome told me about a paper that he needed to write at the end of the summer internship for credit. While cleaning out the evidence room, he came across an evidence bag containing a single bullet. It was the bullet from the Ben Smith armed bank robbery case when Officer Miller was shot in the leg."

"This is making no sense to me," Johns said.

"Well, we received the three bullets that were taken from Dr. Buckle's body . . . ." she started.

"Are you telling me that Jerome sent a bullet from an active murder investigation to Madison in order to write a paper?!" Johns bellowed.

"Yes. Somehow he must have gotten you to sign the authorization," Shirley stammered.

"Christ!" Johns shouted and waved his right hand so wildly that it hit his coffee cup and sent it flying, spilling coffee over the newly formed piles of mail. His face was red.

"Do we still have the gun from the Smith case?"

"No, Jerome couldn't find it."

Johns slumped back into his chair in a state of disbelief. He stared into space for several moments. A pimply faced intern!

"Call Officer Kennickson and tell him to go to Jerome's house and pick him up. I don't care how sick he is. I want to see him here immediately!"

Shirley rushed from the room to make the call. Johns got up from his chair, grabbed the report and paced around the room, re-reading it, oblivious to the coffee slowly dripping from the table to the floor.

Fifteen minutes later, Jerome was standing in front of him. He looked terrible. His nose was red and his eyes were puffy. He was wearing a pair of blue jeans hastily thrown on, pajama tops with pink elephants, penny loafers with no socks and a Vicks-smelling handkerchief wrapped around his neck. In his hand was a wad of disgusting looking tissues. Jerome surveyed the coffee-stained mail on the table and immediately focused on the evidence bag with the two bullets. He went pale. Oh shit!

"Sit down, Jerome," Johns said.

Johns pulled a chair over to the messy desk. Jerome sneezed, apologized and promptly sat down. Oh, God. He was sure that he was going to be fired.

"So, tell me how these two bullets ended up in Madison, and don't leave out the part about my signature authorization!"

Jerome stared down at his shoes and started to speak in a voice just above a whisper. Shirley got him a box of tissues. As Jerome's story unfolded, Johns intently stared at him. He had already worked out in his mind that Jerome had accidentally stumbled onto a crucial piece of evidence. Looking at Jerome suffering through his cold, he felt a little guilty about bringing him in like he did. He needed to go easy on him.

As Jerome slowly told his story, the one thing Johns learned was that he should read what he is signing. It was too easy for Jerome to get his signature. Jerome believed that once the report came back, he could intercept it easily, because the chief was always behind opening his mail.

Shirley gasped and then giggled when Jerome spoke about the chief's mail. Johns ignored her. He saw no humor in this.

Jerome also thought he could replace the missing bullet from Dr. Buckle's evidence bag before anyone missed it.

When Jerome finished speaking, Johns asked if he ever suspected that the two bullets would match. Jerome just shook his head. He had no idea that the gun that shot Officer Miller was also the one that killed Dr. Buckle.

"So where is the gun?" That was the question the chief wanted answered. Jerome just shook his head and blew his nose again. After a long minute of silence, Shirley suggested that the retired janitor, Herbert Hager, was probably the last person to see the gun.

Jerome was now uncontrollably coughing and his nose running. He looked scared. Through his discomfort, he asked the chief if he was fired.

Johns smiled at him. "Hell, no," he said softly, but then forced himself to raise his voice, "but a reprimand seems to be in order."

Wide-eyed, Jerome nodded, thanked the chief and asked Shirley for a ride home. She took him to her office and called Officer Kennickson.

Johns went into his office, sat back in his chair with his eyes closed and mused how a summer intern could inadvertently stumble onto a piece of evidence that could lead to the possible capture and conviction of a murderer. This episode with Jerome reaffirmed his belief that life has its little surprises and one always had to be ready to expect the unexpected.

He needed to reconvene with Sigenthaler and Gates. This investigation suddenly had a new and interesting twist!

CHAPTER 26

Pam Burkhalter was sitting on her living room sofa waiting for Pastor Carl. Dwayne was as comfortable as he could be under the circumstances, resting in his upstairs bedroom. He had been home a week since his court date. Fritz had to help him up the stairs since Dwayne insisted on staying in his own room. Pam had looked in on him a few minutes ago and he was sleeping. This was a good sign, because his doctor said he needed as much rest as possible to make a full recovery.

Dwayne was depressed. After he got home from the court house, he ignored his parents and siblings. He spent a lot of time sitting in his wheel chair, just staring into space and didn't want anyone around him. His favorite spot was the front porch. Pam tried to comfort him, but he pushed her away. Fritz was just as stubborn as his son and kept his distance. When Dwayne was on the porch, Fritz would enter the house through the kitchen door at the back of the house to avoid him. The tension in the house was thick and repressive, and had everyone on edge. Even the younger kids found a reason to be absent from the house.

Pam was heartbroken. She loved her son very much and to see him in this state of mind was killing her. In her heart, she knew Dwayne was innocent. She knew him as well as any mother knows her children, and he wasn't capable of murder! When she reassured him that the family was standing behind him and believed in his innocence, he had no response. She needed to know what was going on inside his head. Whatever it was, he had withdrawn from his family and friends and was now living in his own little world. Years ago, Pam's mother had told her that people always have secrets, and it's only a matter of time to find out what they are. She was hoping that Pastor Carl could help her.

Pam heard the bold tick tock in the abnormally quiet house and glanced at the pendulum clock on the north wall. It was ten forty a.m.; Pastor Carl was running late. She went into the kitchen and brought back a tray of bars and crackers and assorted cheeses that she had prepared. Putting them on the table in front of the sofa, she went back into the kitchen and poured herself a cup of coffee. As she was walking back into the living room, she looked out the picture window and saw Pastor Carl's car speeding up the driveway. He stopped in front of the house, jumped out and hurried to the front porch. She laughed at the sight of him as she met him at the front door.

"I am so sorry for being late," he said. "I have no excuse other than the time just got away from me."

Pam smiled and led him into the living room. After he was seated, she got him a cup of coffee. He picked up a bar and wolfed it down. Pam grinned. It was the first time she had smiled since Dwayne got home.

"I am glad you called," Pastor Carl began. "We have missed you at church."

"Thank you for coming. I am at my wits end, and I needed to talk to someone I can trust. I am worn out trying to reason with my son."

Pastor Carl smiled at her. "Thank you. How can I help?"

"I am so worried for Dwayne. He refuses to have anything to do with the family. After we brought him home, I thought all he needed was his family's support and love. But that hasn't happen. He is withdrawn and angry." Pam's voice was a little shaky. She paused for a moment. She didn't want to cry in front of the pastor. She reached into her dress pocket, pulled out a handwritten note and handed it to Pastor Carl. It read, "Why does it always rain on my birthday?"

"Did Dwayne give you this note?"

"Yes. It's the only communication I've had with him since he came home."

Pastor Carl gave the note back to her.

"I have some concerns that I need to sort out, and I need a good listener. We are alone in the house, expect for Dwayne, who is sleeping upstairs. We can talk freely."

Pastor Carl nodded and took a sip of coffee. He was happy to be so affirmed in his pastoral role. Eyeing the dessert bars again, he reached over and took two more. He leaned back in his chair and prepared himself to give her his full attention.

"First of all, I want to say that Dwayne is innocent of this murder. I know my son, and he is incapable of such a horrific thing. I told him that I believed in his innocence, but he doesn't respond. Except for the note, he just ignores me. That really hurts. I always thought we were close. I also have the feeling that he knows that he is innocent, but there is something else weighing heavily on his mind."

She paused for a moment, but Pastor Carl didn't say anything, so she continued.

"I think Rita Steffes is the underlying cause of his difficulty. Do you know her?"

Pastor Carl said he knew Rita and her family, but not very well.

"When I was pregnant with Dwayne, both Fritz and I were overjoyed. When our first boy was born, we named him after his grandfather. Fritz now had a son that would take over and farm for another generation, just like he did from his father. Dwayne was a happy child and enjoyed following his dad around and helping with chores and just being outside with him.

"Even as a child, Dwayne could be as stubborn as his father. As you know, farming is a tough occupation. Fritz learned from his dad to endure the hardships like a combat soldier, and then soldier on when times got tough. His stubborn determinism has kept us going over the years. The bond between father and son was strong. The expectation that Dwayne would one day get married and take over the farm was never in doubt.

"One funny story I remember was when Dwayne was five years old. We were at a church picnic and the kids were running around. He got too close to a chair and ran straight into it and tumbled to the ground. He quickly jumped up and said in German, "Ziehen Sie den kopf aus dem arsch!" Everyone laughed and looked at Fritz's red face."

Pastor Carl looked puzzled, and Pam blushed. "It means, 'Pull your head out of your ass!'"

Pastor Carl laughed, and Pam used the break in her story to get him another cup of coffee.

"Everything abruptly changed when Dwayne started his junior year of high school." Pam said as she returned. "He was invited to a birthday party for a classmate, and he was suddenly exposed to another world. The classmate was the son of a prominent lawyer in Monroe who lived in a very fine house on 20th Avenue. For the first time in his life, Dwayne saw the excesses that money could buy. He was immediately intimidated and felt some shame for growing up in the country on a farm that practiced austerity. The sight of all the toys and new clothes and stuff overwhelmed him with envy. Also, he realized firsthand the social divide between farm families and city families. The sudden urge to leave the party was overpowering.

"He saw Rita there, and she was the center of attention. She was cute, well groomed, funny, and laughed a lot. Dwayne was instantly taken with her. She was nice enough to him, but he wanted more. He wanted to date her! Coming home from the party had changed him."

Pam looked at the family portrait on the table next to her, and then turned her attention back to Pastor Carl.

"We have a good life here on the farm," she said, "but Dwayne desperately wanted to be accepted into Rita's circle of friends. He saw that other farm kids who played sports, especially football and basketball, could be seen socializing with the city kids. When Dwayne asked his dad to play sports, Fritz would have nothing to do with it. Running the farm and farm chores were to be Dwayne's first priority and that was that. No further discussion. I tried to soften my husband's attitude, but he wouldn't budge. He got into some heated and excitable arguments with Dwayne, but his mind was made up. Fritz didn't play high school sports, so his son didn't need to either."

"Would Dwayne playing high school sports have put a hardship on the farm?" Pastor Carl asked. Pam reflected on his question.

"Other farm kids were doing it. I suppose arrangements could have been made so that the chores would get done. Now that you mention it, maybe this was more about Fritz than Dwayne."

"Just a thought," said Pastor Carl.

"Well, anyway, Dwayne wasn't interested in dating country girls. As his anger and resentment grew, he did something odd. He hung up a punching bag in the machine shed and spent hours pounding on it. He said it made him feel better. He bitterly resented Fritz for standing in his way. It was like he looked over the fence at greener pastures and desperately wanted to go there.

"And then an interesting thing happened. It was like a watershed moment in his young life. He was invited to an after-the-football-game party. Usually these were closed parties at an isolated location with a bonfire, beer and that sort of thing. He was pretty excited about the invite. All he could talk about was seeing Rita there. Looking at her every day in the hallways in high school and never having a chance with her seemed to drive him crazy.

"He got home late from the party, so when I heard him, I went down to the kitchen. I found him cleaning himself up in the kitchen sink. He was a mess. The shirt he was wearing was bloody, and he had cuts on his face and hands. I asked him what happened, and he told me he fell down."

"Did you believe him?" Pastor Carl asked.

"No, I didn't. But he was in a very good mood and almost giddy. He told me Rita kissed him. When I asked what happened and why Rita kissed him, he just smiled and kissed me on the cheek and went to bed. I only found out later about the fight. He beat up the school bully!"

"What happened next?" Pastor Carl asked, riveted and immersed in her story.

"He and Rita started dating. Some of my friends warned me about her, that she had a reputation. I tried to talk to Dwayne, but he wouldn't listen. Just like his dad, he had that stubborn free will!

"All he could talk about were the closed cliquish parties that he and Rita were going to. He told his dad that he was now somebody special. After high school they continued to date, and it seemed to me that Rita was using him. This may seem pejorative, but I think Rita was only looking for a lover and a warrior, and she found both in Dwayne. The bar fights made me sick. It was a high price to pay to keep Rita. He hinted that he wanted to marry her, but I don't think she ever had any intentions to marry him."

"What were Dwayne's expectations? Did he really think he had a chance with Rita?"

"I think he was in a fantasy world when it came to Rita. He was trying to defy gravity, and she kept pulling him down. He felt he was upgrading himself. In his mind, life lived as a city kid would make him happy."

"Did he really believe that Rita would lead him to happiness?"

"Yes, I think he believed that. But when life intervened and burst his fantasy, he fell hard."

"What do you mean?"

"I am saying that Rita betrayed him. She always led him on and was playing with his emotions like some perverted and dark game. The final act of cruelty was when she lied about the night of the murder. When he needed her the most, she abandoned him. A cold heart if there was ever one!"

"Has she tried to contact him since he has been home?"

"No. Nothing. Dwayne just sits and waits and torments himself."

"Has he had any other visitors? Friends or relatives?" Pastor Carl asked.

"Well, yes he has. Bonnie Koss came by to visit Dwayne a couple of times. Do you know her?"

"Yes, her parents farm north of Monroe. From what I hear she has led a difficult life. A nice enough girl, but she has had some bad breaks in her life. Her family attends church in Monticello."

"I think she's nice. We had a pleasant visit after she talked to Dwayne. Well, anyway, she thinks Dwayne is innocent, and she has nothing nice to say about Rita. She told me Rita has birds in her attic!"

Pastor Carl smiled. "Did Dwayne comment on her visits?"

"He hasn't commented on anything!" Pam exploded and then quickly apologized.

"So what do you think about Dwayne's future? As his mother, what do you see?"

"I think he needs to get over Rita. It's obvious that she doesn't care for him. Bonnie has shown more compassion towards him than Rita is capable of. Dwayne's obsession with Rita needs to come to an end. The destructive hold she has over him can't continue. I think his addiction to her will take time to overcome." Finally, Pam felt relieved. She couldn't have had this conversation with her husband.

"I have been here about an hour, and you haven't talked about the murder. Are you truly convinced that Dwayne is innocent?"

"Yes I am! My faith is carrying me through this difficult time. I pray every day to God that Dwayne will heal and be found innocent."

"Can I say a prayer?"

"Thank you," Pam whispered.

Pastor Carl and Pam bowed their heads. He prayed for Pam, Dwayne and the entire family.

CHAPTER 27

In the brightness of a full moon, Attorney Jeff Fouts sped south on Highway 69 to Clarno. He was in a hurry. A few clouds drifted across the night sky causing eerie shadows along the road side, but he didn't seem to notice. He wasn't thinking about deer or any other nocturnal animals that were destined for road kill. His mind was focused on the task at hand.

Dwayne had told him a few minutes earlier where the gun was hidden at his uncle's farm. While visiting Dwayne at his parent's farm, Fouts finally pried out of him the information he so desperately needed. Thank God for Mrs. Burkhalter. She convinced Dwayne to tell him. Why didn't he trust lawyers?

Fouts felt an extreme urgency to get to the farm to find the gun before the police. But as he drove, he had a hard time remembering the exact spot where Dwayne told him it would be. Dwayne was able to talk again, but his speech was somewhat incoherent. His conversation with Dwayne was very short, and he didn't write down all the detailed information. But he felt confident that, once he got to the farm, he could find it. This was exciting news, because once the ballistic tests were run on the gun, Dwayne would be cleared and found innocent. Jeff Fouts would be the hero in the eyes of the community and Diane. Justice served.

About two miles before he came to County Road P, Fouts spotted someone walking along the west side the road. He was wearing a three-quarter length black coat and a Stetson-style hat pulled down over his face. As he sped past the figure, Fouts took a quick glance but didn't recognize him. The hat was covering the figure's face. Fout's quickly surmised that the man's car must have broken down somewhere, and if he wasn't in such a hurry he would have stopped to offer assistance. Besides, he thought a Green

County Sheriff's patrol car should be coming by shortly to help, and he put the strange man out of his thoughts.

Fouts slowed down and turned east on County Road P. He was racking his brain to remember where Dwayne said the gun was. It wasn't like him to forget such a detail. He said it was near the barn somewhere, Fouts thought.

Suddenly an owl appeared from nowhere and flew in front of his car.

"What the hell?" he yelled. Fouts swerved hard to the left to avoid hitting it and screeched to a stop. His heart was beating very fast, and he was shaking badly as he tried to calm his nerves. The wing span on that owl must have been five feet! he thought. The alternating light and dark shadows were playing tricks on him. To the right, he could see the cemetery and a large gray angel partially covered in moss. It was the largest head stone in the cemetery and looked creepy in the shadows.

Fouts began his journey again and slowly made his way through the little community of Clarno. He thought it strange that he hadn't seen or passed another vehicle on this trip. Even the streets of Clarno were deserted.

He refocused his attention on the gun as he picked up speed through the s-curves. The mystery of the missing gun haunted him. What if he gets there and can't find it? He began to sweat a little. Before he realized it, he was traveling seventy miles per hour. In the shadows, he saw what he thought was a deer standing next to the road and slowed down, but it was only a bush. His imagination was getting the better of him.

His car crested a hill and the headlamps shined brightly on an object standing in the middle of the road. What was it? At first he thought it was a deer, but suddenly it seemed more like a human being. Fouts panicked! He was quickly closing in on it. There was no time to stop. Instantly, he realized that he couldn't avoid hitting whatever it was. He jumped hard on the brakes.

The clouds parted just before impact, and he saw all the horror happening in slow motion. It was a man wearing what looked like a Stetson hat. The sound of the impact was awful. The man flew up over the hood of his car and hit the windshield. In a split second, he had disappeared over the top of the car. Quickly looking into his rear view mirror, Fouts saw him land on the road behind the car.

Suddenly, his car swerved erratically, and he lost control. The tires squealed on the county blacktop, and then hit the soft shoulder of the road. The car skidded sideways down into a deep ditch. Fouts felt the car turning over and over as it smashed against shrubs, fence posts, rocks and small trees. He held tightly onto the steering wheel. He was being tossed around inside the car as if he was in a washing machine. Loud scraping sounds pierced his hearing. And then he blacked out.

When he came to again, Fouts realized the car was still and lying on its side. He smelled pungent dirt and its odor of decay inside the car. He could hear one of the tires spinning. He was dazed. His face was wet with blood, and his upper lip felt like it had split in two. The taste of blood was in his mouth. Through the blood and sweat and dirt on his face, he could barely see the driver's side window was busted out above him. He tried to move, but couldn't. Fear and panic began to consume his very being. He felt very dizzy and faint, as if he would lose consciousness at any moment. He couldn't believe what had just happened. Was he going to die?

Fouts tried to make another movement with his arm. Nothing happened. He had no feeling whatsoever in his limbs. Was he paralyzed? He was beginning to grow faint once again. Then, suddenly, he was aware of someone or something at the driver's side window looking down at him. "Help me, please help me," he pleaded in a faint voice through the pain and his tears.

He could now see a human face at the window. Through his own impaired vision, he could see the face staring down at him was also covered in blood. The face just silently stared at him. Again he pleaded for help.

Then he saw a hand with droplets of blood dripping from its fingers slowly reach inside the window toward him. The red droplets hit his lips and slipped into his mouth. The blood had a metallic taste. Fouts instantly went into a state of panic. He gasped for breath trying to stave off the mounting terror. He could barely speak as wave after wave of despair and terror washed over him in a torrent of horror!

The clouds suddenly parted again, and for an instant the full moon shone fully on the bloodied face of Dr. Andrew Buckle. Fouts was staring at a ghost—a creature from hell! It had no eyes, only bottomless empty sockets.

Fouts screamed as loudly as he could and tried frantically to escape. He was trapped! The bloodied hand was almost to his face as he screamed louder and louder. Sweat and sheer terror flowed out of every pore of his body. The ghoulish hand reached his cheek and touched him! His scream was so loud it woke him up. Fouts was tightly tangled in his sheets and drowning in sweat. It took him a full ten minutes to compose himself. The nightmare unhinged him.

CHAPTER 28

Sigenthaler drove his patrol car at the posted speed limit, headed north on Highway 81 toward Argyle. Once there, he would turn on County Road G and follow it to Yellowstone Lake in Blanchardville.

Chief Johns had given him the assignment to interview Herbert Hager. Sigenthaler found out from Hager's son that Hager and his wife were camping at Yellowstone Lake State Park for the week.

As he cruised along, he felt disappointed and upset. Jerome's findings had offered up an alternate theory of the crime. The chief had jumped on this new information and was excited. Sigenthaler still thought that Burkhalter was the killer and somehow the gun that shot Officer Miller had come into his possession. Sigenthaler stubbornly held onto his theory; he was hoping that Hager could somehow confirm it. After all his bravado at the PD, he needed to save face.

It was a beautiful sunny morning for the short trip from Monroe. He had his driver's side window open to feel the cool breeze on his face. On any other day, he would have enjoyed the ride through the rolling pastoral hills of southern Wisconsin. But today, the fields and rows of corn and the Holsteins out in their pastures went unobserved. The manicured lawns of the farm places and the fresh paint on the barns he ignored. Today he was eager to get to the lake and was lost in his thoughts as he tightly gripped the steering wheel.

After a long search for the gun at the Harold Burkhalter farm in Clarno, he and Deputy Swensen finally found it at the bottom of the abandoned well. Sigenthaler was thrilled about the find and, with a puffed-out chest, couldn't wait to give it to the chief to receive a big 'atta boy' for his efforts. But that didn't happen. The Chief thanked him for finding Dwayne Burkhalter's gun and said he would send it to Madison for a ballistics check. Johns then proceeded to tell him and Gates about another theory of the murder. After filling them in on the two bullets and the report from the Crime Lab, the chief was convinced that Jerome had accidentally cracked the case.

As Sigenthaler neared his destination, he was starting to second-guess his own theory. What had once seemed so clear to him was now falling apart at the seams and filling him with doubts. Had he jumped to his theory of the murder too soon without considering all the facts? Was Gates right in challenging him? He was angry at himself and embarrassed. He should have known better and kept his mouth shut. His fellow officers won't let him forget this one if he is proven wrong. The singular thought on his mind now was to find out if Hager remembered what happened to the gun. He also realized that the chief could be right, and Hager's information could possibly lead them to the killer.

As he turned onto County Road G, fond memories of Yellowstone Lake interrupted his thoughts. The lake was man-made, covering about 455 acres. The park had plenty of recreational opportunities including camping, swimming, boating, fishing and hiking. The fishing was outstanding. The lake was stocked with crappies, walleye, bass, bluegill, catfish, muskies and northern pike. Sigenthaler had spent many wonderful weekends there with his dad in the family fishing boat. It was always the most relaxing time of his life. In the winter, they would go ice fishing. During family reunions, they would share funny stories about their adventures on the lake. He especially liked the story about his dad losing his fishing pole to a big fish and then falling out of the boat. For a man who said he couldn't swim, his dad sure made it back into the boat in record time. Years later when he thought about it, a smile always came to his face.

Sigenthaler eased his patrol car to a stop in front of the camp registration office. Kids were scampering around everywhere, and campers with their dogs on leashes passed him by. A small convenience store with food, pop, ice and other sundries was next to the office. It was full of campers. In fact, the whole park was over flowing with people. Some of them stopped to look at his patrol car, and some the kids stared at him.

Inside the office, he asked the elderly attendant for the campsite number for the Hagers. The man had short gray hair, a missing front tooth and a pot belly. He looked to be in his seventies. As he opened the card registration box, Sigenthaler noticed a stub finger and concluded, probably a retired farmer. Thumbing through the index cards, the whiskered man seemed to be in no hurry. The cards weren't alphabetized, so he started at the front of the box and slowly worked his way back. Sigenthaler waited patiently. Finally, the attendant took a card out of the box and handed it to him. "Is this the fella you're lookin' for?"

Sigenthaler glanced at the card and nodded. The card read "Hager—Campsite # 27" in big bold red letters. He thanked the man and handed the card back. He noticed the attendant put the card in the front of the box. Sigenthaler went back to his car and drove slowly along a gravel road to campsite #27, which took him past the swimming beach area. Kids and adults were swimming and splashing in the roped-off area. The lake was calm and beautiful. He saw about a dozen fishing boats and, for a brief moment, wished he could be out there with them. He also saw about a dozen picnic tables along the shore with people sitting at them, eating picnic lunches and enjoying themselves.

Seeing a sign with an arrow that indicated #27 was to the right, he turned and followed a gravel road back into the trees. Immediately to his left, he spotted a white cinder block building that housed warm showers, flush toilets and sinks with mirrors. He always thought this was a pretty modern campground. Before he knew it, he spotted #27 and stopped, got out of his patrol car and made his way to a ballooned-out tent camper.

As he approached the camper, he saw a very plump older woman, with bluish-dyed hair wearing Bermuda shorts and a Green Bay Packer tee shirt, fast asleep on a chaise lounge chair. Her glasses sat on the tip of her nose, and an old copy of Life magazine lay in her lap. She had bare feet with pink painted toe nails. The rhythmic snoring from her open mouth was loud. Sigenthaler stopped and stared at her, not knowing whether to wake her up.

He glanced around the campsite and saw a Weber grill, a fire pit with cut wood piled up, a blue food chest and a five-gallon container of potable water. Next to the woman was a table with rust on the legs and two chairs parked under a canopy.

Suddenly and without warning, she opened her eyes! Sigenthaler jumped when she bellowed, "Who are you?" She remained in her lounge chair and adjusted her glasses.

Sigenthaler explained that he was from the Monroe Police Department and was looking for Mr. Herbert Hager, because they were conducting an ongoing investigation, and he had a few questions for Mr. Hager.

"Do you want a beer?" she asked. He declined.

"Is my husband a suspect?"

Sigenthaler laughed. "No. I just want to ask him a couple of questions."

"Well he ain't here. He's out fishing out on the lake, but he should be back shortly. Do you want to wait for him?"

Sigenthaler thought about it for a moment. "No. I'll just go down to the boat launch and wait for him to come in. Thank you for your help."

"Anything else I can help you with?" she asked.

"No, thank you," he said, and excused himself.

Sigenthaler followed the signed arrows back through the trees to the boat docking area.

He parked and walked over to a vacant picnic table near the dock. He settled in to wait. From what he remembered about Herbert Hager, he was like an invisible man who was there and wasn't there at the same time while working at the police station. He was a fixture much like a desk or table lamp. Hager never talked much, so he was taken for granted and unseen. The officers pretty much ignored him as he cleaned up the trash, polished the floors, performing light maintenance and any other assigned tasks. He was friendly enough but very quiet. He must have been retired three months before Sigenthaler realized he was gone.

After a little while, Sigenthaler saw a small aluminum fishing boat slowly working its way toward the dock. Even from a distance, he recognized Hager—he was wearing a green John Deere implement cap. Sigenthaler waved to him, and Hager waved back. As he got closer, Hager cut his 20 hp motor and drifted in the last few feet before he tied up his boat to the dock. He climbed out with a stringer of pan fish that glistened in the sun. He was wearing a scruffy pair of brown shoes, blue jeans with holes in the knees, a Hawaiian flowered shirt and a week's worth of whiskers.

Sigenthaler suddenly remembered another police officer, who had gone to Hager's retirement party, said Hager, in his short speech, stated that in retirement he had only two worries: One was running out of cigarettes and the other was running of beer.

They met at the end of the dock and exchanged greetings. Hager's voice was raspy from a lifelong addition to cigarettes. Sigenthaler told him about the short visit he had with his wife, who directed him to the dock.

Hager smiled. "Ain't she a thing of beauty?"

Sigenthaler was momentarily speechless. Fortunately, Hager didn't wait for an answer.

"What can I do for you, seeing that you drove all the way from Monroe to see me? Am I in any kind of trouble?" Then he laughed.

Sigenthaler filled him in with as much information as he could, without revealing the sensitive particulars of the investigation. Then he got specific and asked if he remembered the Smith case. Hager furrowed his eyebrows, squinted his eyes and nodded. Sigenthaler had his full attention.

"The reason I am here is that the gun from that case is missing from the evidence room, and I need to know if you remember what happened to it."

Hager screwed up his face and remained silent. It was as if he was thinking about one of the Seven Wonders of the World. "Well, give me a minute," he said. After about two minutes, Sigenthaler was getting anxious. He had the impression he was being played.

"I'll tell you what," Hager finally said, "for twenty dollars I think my memory would get better."

"What!" Sigenthaler exploded and stared at him with an open mouth. "Look, this is a murder inquiry, and I don't have the time for games!"

Hager rocked back and forth on his worn out shoes and smiled. Another minute went by. He knew he had Sigenthaler where he wanted him. "I think I remember giving the gun to someone, but I will need some time to remember to whom."

Sigenthaler was incensed. His mind was racing. If he threatened him, Hager would know the cop didn't have a case against him. He also realized that he was beaten and begrudgingly reached into his pants pocket, took out a ten dollar bill and handed it to Hager. "That's all you'll get from me this side of jail sentence in the county jail, you little miser!"

Hager snatched the money from Sigenthaler's hand. He looked at it, smelled it and then stuffed it into his pants pocket.

"I gave the gun to that lawyer fella, Jeff Fouts."

"What?" Sigenthaler immediately questioned.

"A year after that Smith guy went to prison, I was in Baumgartners having a beer and Limburger cheese sandwich, when this Fouts comes in and sits down next to me. I knew who he was, but we had never spoken before. We struck up a casual conversation, and I tell him that the police chief wants me to clean out the evidence room. There was about a twenty-year supply of junk stored there, and he wanted it all cleaned out. Fouts asked me if the gun used in the Smith case was still there. I told him it was, and he offered to pay me twenty-five dollars for it. He said he wanted to keep it as a memento of the bank robbery. Since the chief wasn't very specific about getting rid of the stuff, I gave it to him."

"Did he give you the full twenty-five dollars?"

Hager smiled.

Sigenthaler couldn't believe what he was hearing. He quickly said good-bye and left Hager standing on the dock. As he was walking back to his car, Hager yelled after him. "That limp looks pretty serious. I'm willing to bet you ten dollars that you will need a walking cane before you retire!" Hager doubled over in laughter.

Sigenthaler ignored him. He jumped back into his patrol car and raced back to Monroe.

CHAPTER 29

Diane Fouts was alone in her red brick house located in the 1700 block of 8th Street, a couple of blocks off the downtown square. Detective Gates would be at her door at ten a.m. to interview her. She was standing in front of a full length mirror in her upstairs bedroom. The face looking back at her was tired and worried. A few wrinkles were noticeable around her eyes. The impending interview with the detective had made her very nervous. She was wearing a loose fitting blue cotton dress and sandals. After her sexual assault, she had lost twenty pounds and looked thin. Her auburn hair was tied back in a bun. A little bit of mascara and lipstick highlighted her face. She momentarily closed her eyes to steady herself and then went down stairs to the kitchen.

The kids were at St. Michael's for the morning. She was glad they were away so they wouldn't be home when Gates arrived. Too many questions would be asked.

The light lunch she prepared included a small cheese tray and freshly baked oatmeal cookies. Fresh fruit from the refrigerator added purple grapes, pineapple wedges and orange slices to the morning repast. The aroma of fresh brewed coffee permeated the kitchen and living room. Satisfied all was ready, Diane went into the living room to wait. She seated herself on a green striped sofa, facing the street and peering out the picture window, anxiously watching for Gates to arrive. The time was nine forty-five a.m.

The house seemed empty and cold to her. After Jeff moved out, the warm feeling of family, home and hearth disappeared. The sounds of laughter and joy were gone. The gloom and despair of separation had settled in. Even the kids seemed to notice the change. If it wasn't for the kids, she felt she would go crazy. Her only really true and trusted friend was Julie Stryker. She was an amazing woman who could comfort her in her darkest hours. Diane felt very safe in the protective cocoon of her friendship and loyalty. And now she was about to be interviewed by a police officer about one of the most horrific and embarrassing physical attacks against her person in her entire lifetime. The humiliation she felt was unbearable.

Diane asked herself over and over again whether she should have done something differently. Seeing Dr. Buckle on the second floor of the hospital almost daily and smiling and talking to him was haunting her. Did she send him the wrong message? Did he mistake her friendliness for something else? She hadn't been aware of any personal danger or broken trust between them. Julie constantly told her that what happened to her wasn't her fault. Nevertheless, she felt guilty, isolated and alone. The shame of it made her feel that she was damaged and couldn't face the public and especially her co-workers. How could that beast of a man demean her is such a way to rob her of her dignity and pride. The assault had left her emotionally wounded and scarred.

From her sofa, she saw the patrol car pull up and stop in front of her house. She saw Detective Gates exit the car and make her way up the sidewalk. She got up from the sofa and went to the front door to greet her. On the way, she offered up a quick prayer to help her get through the interview.

After Gates was seated in an overstuffed arm chair next to the sofa, Diane went to the kitchen and returned with the trays of food and two cups of steaming black coffee. She placed them on the Queen Anne table in front of the sofa. After she was seated again, she smiled timidly at Sam. Sam helped herself to a couple of slices of aged cheddar cheese and a cookie and placed them on a small etched glass plate. The cheese was delicious. They sipped their coffee.

"Thank you for seeing me today," Sam began. "I know this must be painful for you, but I need to ask you a few questions." Diane nodded looking down at the cheese tray.

"How well did you know Dr. Buckle?"

The question unhinged her. The fear and tension in her body erupted. "She knows!" Then for the next fifteen minutes she told Gates about the rape. She was sweating as her shrill voice recounted the whole sordid affair. She talked non-stop. Gates stared at her stone faced. This was much more than she expected. After Diane finished she slumped back on the sofa. They both remained silent. Then Diane stood up and excused herself. She went into the half bath off the living room and washed her face.

Sam also needed the time to recover. This was a shocking development. Suddenly a thought flashed through her mind. "Did Diane kill Dr. Buckle?" Then, just as fast, she dismissed it. Her gut instinct told her to leave it alone for now.

When Diane returned she smiled weakly at Gates. "Sorry about that," she said. She sat down again and sipped her cold coffee.

"Just to put your mind at ease, I am not going to ask you any questions or intimate details about your sexual assault."

A sense of relief immediately flooded over Diane. She visibly relaxed. The tension in her neck and shoulders went away. She sat back comfortably on the sofa and looked at Sam.

"Thank you," she said.

"As you are aware, we are looking for the killer of Dr. Buckle. We thought you may have some information that you aren't aware of. A small, seemingly insignificant detail has solved many criminal cases. I just want you to relax and reflect on Dr. Buckle and anyone who may have held a grievance against him. Since his murder, have any thoughts or ideas come to you as who may have killed him?"

Diane wrinkled her nose and was lost in thought for a few moments. Was there something she saw or heard that may help the detective? Sam patiently sipped her coffee and waited.

"No, no one I can think of, to be perfectly honest with you. Of course, Rita's boyfriend is on everyone's lips. But, aside from that, I have no idea."

Then, suddenly, without any warning, Diane exploded. "I'm glad he's dead! That bastard ruined my life!" A tear instantly appeared and trickled down her left cheek. She wiped it away.

Sam was dumbstruck. This sudden outburst was totally unexpected. Watching her wipe away the tear, she realized how close to the edge Diane was living her life. She felt sorry for her. This interview was hard on Sam, but she knew it was part of her job and had to be done.

"I understand," Sam replied and waited for Diane to compose herself. "How many people have you told about the assault?"

Diane picked up a cookie and took a bite.

"The only ones I have told are Julie Stryker and my husband. But you know how gossip gets wings and flies around Monroe."

Sam smiled. She knew only too well. "How did they react when you told them?"

"Well, Julie is a saint. She has rallied around me and supported me in every possible way. I don't know what I would have done without her. Her compassion and caring has kept me together and sane. I trust her more than any other living person." She paused and finished the oatmeal cookie on her plate and took another sip of coffee.

"How did your husband take the news?"

"As you probably know, we're separated."

Sam nodded.

"He came to see me the day after it happened. He brought me flowers in an attempt to win me back after what he did to me. He can be such a bastard! Does he think that flowers can erase the pain and suffering of two affairs? Well, anyway, I was surprised to see him. After the assault, I must have taken a dozen showers. When he arrived, I had just stepped out of the shower. I met him at the front door. He could see my nervousness and distress. He was very insistent to know why I was so upset. He followed me back up stairs to the bedroom, and I showed him the bruises on my neck and arms."

"What did he say? What did he do?"

Diane put her coffee cup down. Her hands were shaking, and she clasped them tightly together.

"He went crazy. He started to act out. He wanted to know who did that to me. I told him Dr. Buckle had assaulted me at the hospital. Immediately he demanded to know all the details. He wanted to know if I had reported the assault to the police. I told him no. He got really upset and threatened to go the police and report it himself. I told him not to go to the police. He got even angrier. I told him that he had already screwed up my life enough and to just leave me alone." Diane paused. She looked down at her feet.

"What happened next?"

"He said some threatening things about Dr. Buckle and raced down the stairs and out of the house."

"Did you take the threats seriously?"

"Not really. Jeff has a quick temper and has a habit of shooting off his mouth when he's upset."

"Have you talked to him since he left that day?"

"He called me a couple of times, but I put him off. My mental state is very fragile right now. Julie constantly reminds me that I am dealing with two of life's worst tragedies at the same time. The first being an adulterous husband and the second being raped. How can men be so cruel to women and cause us all this pain?!"

Sam sat quietly looking at her. Then the tears started flowing down

Diane's cheeks again in a steady stream. It was as if she had held back her emotions as long as she could, and now they all came gushing out. Sam jumped up and went to sit down beside her on the sofa. She put her arms around Diane and held her tightly as she sobbed uncontrollably. The tears flowed unabated onto her cotton dress and left wet stains.

After a couple minutes, the tears stopped. Diane wiped her cheeks with both hands. Mascara had run down her cheeks. She stood up and apologized and said she would be back. Diane then disappeared up the flight of stairs to her bedroom.

Alone in the living room, Sam walked to the fireplace mantle and looked at two, nicely framed, eight-by-ten family pictures. The photos were probably taken out west somewhere, because they were all dressed up in western clothing. One picture had a stagecoach in the background. The other had horses as a backdrop. The kids looked to be either three or four years old.

Diane came down the stairs and seemed to be under control. She smiled at Sam. She had changed into a pair of blue jeans and a white polo shirt and had cleaned up her face.

"I'm so sorry," Diane said. "I just lost it."

"No need to apologize. I can't imagine the strain you're under."

Diane joined Sam at the fireplace.

"I was just admiring these pictures of your family," Sam said.

"The pictures remind me of happier times. Jeff went through a phase, when the kids were younger, about the old west. He read a book about Judge Roy Bean and fell in love with it. I tried to tell him it was all fantasy and myth, but he wouldn't listen. He told the kids about frontier justice and court sessions being held in saloons. He explained to them that the judge was the "Law West of the Pecos" in west Texas. And he laughed when he frightened them by saying the judge's philosophy was "Hang 'em first, try 'em later.""

Sam smiled.

"We took some family vacations out west. The trips to Rodeo Days in Cheyenne, Wyoming, were his favorites. The kids loved it when he dressed them up in western outfits— as you can see by the pictures! I told him he looked ridiculous when he bought a cowboy hat and duster to wear around Monroe. After a couple of years, he lost interest, and he packed away all his western gear.

Sam stared at the man with his cowboy hat and duster in the picture. Could it be . . ., or could it be too much of a coincidence? She knew she needed to get back to the police station and brief Chief Johns right away. Sam thanked Diane for her time. Diane showed her to the door.

"Sorry I couldn't have been of more help. But quite honestly, I have no idea who killed Dr. Buckle.

CHAPTER 30

Chief Johns was seated alone in the interview room at the police station looking at his notes. The room was small and windowless. A gray rectangle interview table was surrounded by four metal chairs, two on each side. A tape recording device lay in the middle. The walls were painted light gray without any pictures, only a two-way mirror on the east wall. The overhead florescent light was glaring, giving the whole room an empty depressing feel. Just being in there could incite the same images as one of those nightmares that seem to have no end.

The temperature was a cool sixty-five degrees. Some of the officers compared it to a tomb. Sometimes, under the bright lights, the room exuded an eerie feeling to it. And sometimes a suspect's breathing was altered, as if the stale air was suffocating him. There was only one way out of the room, and a police officer would stand at the door blocking any ideas of an escape. Even the detectives who interviewed suspects in there found it gloomy.

Johns thought this would be a good place to meet, because it was quiet and isolated from the rest of the station. Gates and Sigenthaler were to meet him at two p.m. to debrief their interviews with Diane Fouts and Herbert Hager. Sigenthaler had called him and told him about the gun Hager sold to Jeff Fouts. This was the "Aha" moment that Johns had been waiting for! He was excited, now that the investigation could be coming to a close. The thought of getting Nussbaum off his back made him giddy. He hated self-serving, want-to-be politicians! As his mind raced, the idea of a long vacation with Beth without the kids made him smile. He loved police work, but this was the best part-catching the bad guy!

It had been six weeks since the murder, and he was convinced that the killer would be arrested today. He was anxious to hear what Sam had to report from her interview with Mrs. Fouts.

Johns felt sorry for the Burkhalter family. After Dwayne's arrest, public opinion turned against them. The gossip was at a fever pitch. It seemed no one gave Dwayne the benefit of the doubt. His reputation as a hard-nosed fighter didn't do him any favors. The fact that he was being held over for trial must mean he is guilty, or at least that's what people assumed. All the tongue wagging cast a long dark shadow over the city, which extended to the Burkhalter farm.

The embarrassment and humiliation was unbearable for the family. They all stayed close to the farm and went out only when it was absolutely necessary. A few friends dropped by from time to time to check on them and give them support. Mrs. Burkhalter prayed every day for the strength to pull them through. They all believed Dwayne to be innocent after he pleaded with them to believe that he did not kill the doctor. They were confident that their son would be found innocent but, nevertheless, their lives would be changed forever.

Johns wrote the name Jeff Fouts on his note pad and circled it several times. He didn't know very much about him, except for his marital difficulties. Since Diane was such an active member of St. Michael's and well known in the community, the two affairs were common knowledge. Diane had lots of support from her church friends, but Jeff's infidelity didn't seem to bother him or he just didn't care. The pejorative gossip pegged him as some sort of a "middle-aged sexual athlete."

Just as the clock struck two, there was a light knock on the door, and Gates and Sigenthaler entered. They greeted the chief with smiles and sat down at the interview table. They were both twitching with excitement. They wanted to tell their stories.

Johns told Sigenthaler to go first. Sigenthaler spoke rapidly, in a slightly higher pitched voice, like a child relating some exciting news to a parent. No one said anything as he recounted his interview with Hager. Johns only shook his head at the cavalier comments from Hager about the chief paying little attention as Hager cleaned out the evidence room and the sale of the gun. His thoughts drifted back to Jerome and his take on the chief.

Gates went next. She said that she didn't think Diane Fouts was involved in the murder. She was dealing with extreme emotional distress and didn't have the will or capacity to kill anyone. Then she went on to tell about the family pictures taken out west. The pictures showed Jeff Fouts wearing a cowboy hat and duster. Both the chief and Sigenthaler looked at each other.

"Am I hearing what I think I am hearing?" Johns said.

"Yes. The interview with Mrs. Keegan as an eye witness account of a possible suspect wearing a cowboy hat and duster seems to be accurate," Sam responded. "I think it is more than a coincidence."

Sigenthaler was getting antsy. He stood up and sat back down again. Johns told him to be still.

Johns placed his elbows on the table, steepled his index fingers and looked at them. "We have more than enough to go on, in my opinion. We have a connection with the murder weapon and Fouts. We also have a connection of what the suspected killer was wearing the night of the murder."

Both Gates and Sigenthaler nodded in agreement.

"Does anyone disagree or have any opinions or questions?" Johns asked.

They both shook their heads.

"Then we are in agreement. We need to immediately go and pick him up for questioning. Do you think Mrs. Fouts is in any danger?"

"I don't know," Sam said. "We know that Fouts got really angry when Diane told him about the rape. He probably doesn't know that he is a suspect. But if he found out, he may want to contact her."

"I agree that we need to act now," Johns interrupted. "I want you to go to his office and invite him to come down to the station to be interviewed. Then we will contact Mrs. Fouts and inform her about the investigation and her husband's possible involvement."

"What if he isn't at his office?" Sigenthaler asked.

"Well, his receptionist should know where he is. I think he lives in an apartment, so get the address and go there if needed. We need to move on this quickly, so I am not telling Roger Nussbaum until we have Jeff Fouts in custody. He will not be happy about a respected lawyer in Monroe being arrested!"

CHAPTER 31

Jeff Fouts sat slumped back in the leather chair behind his desk at his law office, staring at the pendulum clock on the wall. His face had a blank expression. The sound of the 'tick tock, tick tock' seemed louder than usual. It was one fifteen p.m., and he had just gotten off the phone with his wife. He had called to ask her to get a babysitter, so they could go out for a nice dinner at a white-table-clothed restaurant in Madison tonight. She declined and then proceeded to tell him about the visit from Detective Gates earlier that morning.

Fouts was instantly alarmed. He didn't want to put her off with aggressive questioning, so he controlled his voice and mustered up all the Mr. Nice Guy approach that he could. He wanted to know if Gates asked any questions about him. Diane told him that Gates wanted to know his reaction after she told him about the sexual assault, especially after she showed him the bruises.

"What did you tell her?" he asked.

"I told her that you got very angry and made threats. Then I followed up with that you fly off the handle at times and the threats didn't mean anything."

"Did she believe you? I mean did she ask any other questions?"

"She asked me if I had any idea who the killer might be."

"What did you say?"

"I told her I didn't know. Why do you ask? Is there something you aren't telling me?"

"Oh, no, I was just curious. Tell me again why she visited you this morning."

"She just wanted to know if I had any information or ideas about who could have killed Dr. Buckle."

"What did you tell her?"

"Other than Dwayne Burkhalter, I have no idea who killed Dr. Buckle."

"Did anything else happen while she was there?"

"Well, yes, something curious happened. I only thought about it after she left. She was looking at the pictures on the fireplace mantle with us all dressed up in western clothes. I think she was intently staring at you. You know the pictures that had you dressed up in a cowboy hat and that duster you keep in your closet. She pointed a finger at you and said you looked very authentic in your western clothes."

Fouts instantly felt the hairs on the back of his neck tingle. His hand held a death grip on the phone. His mind was racing as he panicked. As calmly as he could, he told Diane that he had another call and quickly got off the phone. He was suddenly afraid. His heart was beating fast, and his palms were sweaty. He narrowed his eyebrows as he stared at the opposite wall. The police have an eye witness!

A sense of dread and fear overcame him. He acutely realized he was in imminent danger. He got up from his desk and paced around the room. He was sure that the police would come looking for him. He needed time to think.

He went to the two-drawer file cabinet next to his desk and unlocked it. From the second drawer he retrieved the gun that he knew would be there. He looked at it in his hand. The cold steel felt somehow reassuring. He slipped on his suit jacket and placed the gun in the right hand pocket. He tidied up his desk and quickly left his office. As he headed for the front door, he told Dorothy to cancel all his appointments for the rest of the day. Then he disappeared through the door before she could respond.

Fouts walked the short distance to his car and drove off. The only place he could think to go was Twining Park. The park was a short ride from his office. As he turned off 14th Avenue into the park entrance, he noticed kids playing on the ball diamond. He crept along the paved road. Off to his right, he saw a mother watching her children on the jungle gym bars and swings. It was a beautiful day to be in the park. He drove slowly past the F 86D Sabre Jet Interceptor on display. He stopped the car at the Swiss Band Shelter, where the city band often performed. The colorful coats of arms of the cantons of Switzerland decorated the opening of the shelter.

Fouts laid his head back on his car seat and closed his eyes. He needed time to think. But he was too twitchy and nervous. He got out of his car and walked a short distance to the benches in front of the band shelter and sat down. A soft summer breeze blew through his hair.

All he could think about was his gun. Diane probably forgot that he had it, but if the police questioned her about it, she would easily remember it. She was very upset when he brought it home, and she didn't want it in the house.

He felt his life being compressed under the burden of regret and remorse. He began to ask himself what had happened to make him so sinister and deadly. The reason for killing Buckle was starting to haunt him, like trying to solve an indecipherable puzzle. He suddenly felt as though he was riding a galloping horse that he couldn't control. His breathing was labored, and he was still sweating profusely. He needed to see Diane—and see her now!

Fouts ran back to his car and sped out of the park to his house and Diane.

CHAPTER 32

ates and Sigenthaler were excited and apprehensive as they pulled up in front of Fouts' Law Office in their patrol car. They were convinced that he was the killer, and bringing him in for questioning had the blood surging through their veins. The adrenaline rush they felt was invigorating. All their senses were in overdrive.

As they entered through the front door, Dorothy looked up from her desk and smiled at them.

"Can I help you?" she asked.

Sam quickly glanced around the room.

"Yes, thank you. We are here to see Mr. Fouts, if he is available."

Dorothy looked at them suspiciously.

"Do you have an appointment?"

"No, we don't. We just need to talk to him."

Sigenthaler was swaying from side to side. He wanted to get on with it and stop all this chit chat.

"Well, Mr. Fouts isn't here. He left a short while ago."

Sigenthaler stopped swaying and let out a sigh.

"Do you know where he went?" Sam asked.

Dorothy hesitated. She felt extreme loyalty to the firm and was very uncomfortable with these questions. The other two partners were at a conference in Milwaukee, so she was on her own. However, the two police officers in front of her made her extremely nervous.

"When Mr. Fouts left, he didn't say where he was going."

Sam thought about this for a moment.

"What kind of mood was he in when he left the office? I mean, was he relaxed or did he seem anxious to you."

Dorothy hesitated for a moment.

"He was in a hurry. He told me to cancel all his appointments for the afternoon. I assumed that he wasn't coming back."

"Did he say anything else?"

"No. Like I said, he was in a big hurry and just rushed past me."

"Do you have his home address? I mean the address for the apartment where he is currently living?"

Dorothy was now sweating. The two police officers in front of her seemed threatening as they pressed her for information. With a trembling hand, she went through the address Rolodex on her desk, wrote down the address and gave it to Sam. Sam thanked her and started to leave. Then she turned around and faced Dorothy.

"If Mr. Fouts comes back to the office today, please tell him that we are looking for him."

Dorothy nodded. Sigenthaler followed Sam out the door and back to the awaiting patrol car.

They both felt deflated and disappointed. Sam told Sigenthaler the address as he started the car. The drive to the 700 block of 12th Avenue was short. Sigenthaler parked in an empty space in front of the two-story apartment complex. Fouts lived on the second floor, in apartment #16. They knocked at the door, but no one answered. They weren't too surprised.

An elderly woman opened the door across the hallway and looked at them. She was in her eighties and supported by a walking cane.

"Are you looking for Mr. Fouts?"

"Yes, we are. Have you seen him recently?" Sam asked.

"He left for work about eight this morning, and I haven't seen him since."

"If you do see him again, please tell him that the police are looking for him and to contact us."

"Why? Did he do something wrong?"

Sam gasped. Too much information.

"No. He may have some information that could help us, and that's why we are looking for him."

The old woman seemed relieved.

"Okay, I will tell him."

Back in the car, Sam and Sigenthaler talked about their next move. Where could he be?

Sam suggested they go see Mrs. Fouts. Maybe she would know

where they could find him. She gave Sigenthaler directions to the house.

They rang the doorbell and a middle-aged woman answered. She smiled at them and identified herself as the baby sitter.

"We are looking for Mrs. Fouts. Is she at home?" Sam asked.

"No, she isn't here. She had an appointment to see the priest at St. Michael's this afternoon and asked me to watch the kids."

"What time was the appointment?"

"She left about forty-five minutes ago."

"Okay, thanks."

As they were walking back to the patrol car, the woman called out to them.

"Mr. Fouts was here about fifteen minutes ago looking for Diane."

They both stopped in their tracks. Sam spun around and hurried back to the woman.

"What did you tell him?"

"I told him the same thing I told you."

"How did he seem to you? Was he calm?"

"No. He yelled at me when I told him Diane wasn't here. I think he was blaming me for her not being home. He just lost it."

"Did you tell him where she was?"

"Yes I did. That was okay, wasn't it?"

Sam ignored her question and looked at Sigenthaler. Oh shit! She turned and hurried back down the sidewalk with Sigenthaler in tow. Sigenthaler gunned the engine and squealed the tires as he sped down 8th Street and turned onto 20th Avenue, racing for St. Michael's.

CHAPTER 33

Diane Fouts entered the front door of St. Michael's church and made her way to the secretary's office. Mrs. Hansen greeted her with her usual friendly welcome. Mrs. Hansen was an elderly volunteer who watched the desk in the afternoons. She did some filing and answered the phone, but mostly she enjoyed the congregants who would stop by the church to visit. After her husband died, the church provided her the fellowship and warmth she needed. This afternoon she and Father Bernard were alone in the church.

Diane told her she had an appointment with Father Bernard. They chatted briefly, and then Mrs. Hansen left to tell Father Bernard he had a visitor. After a few moments, she returned and told Diane that Father Bernard was on the phone and would be with her shortly. Mrs. Hansen offered her a cup of coffee, but Diane declined. She welcomed this interlude and reflected on what she would tell the priest. Mrs. Hansen returned to her desk, picked up a letter opener and started sorting through today's mail. Diane stood in the doorway and absently watched her.

Diane's decision to make the appointment with the priest was hard. If she was totally honest with herself, she blamed Father Mark for his advice to forgive Jeff. She fully appreciated Catholic guilt and its implications, but she ignored her gut feeling about leaving Jeff after the first affair. The affair had damaged their relationship more than she realized or imagined. She couldn't trust him after that. Her repeated efforts to convince herself otherwise ate at her soul like a mild acid. The children were the rationale that made any real sense to her. They needed a father. After all, other women had stayed with their husbands under similar circumstances and survived. The problem was that she needed someone to love and who would love her back. Jeff was not the man to do that. She needed to talk to the priest to spin out all of her painful feelings. Nevertheless, her mind was made up to leave Jeff!

As to the rape, that was an entirely different matter. She even surprised herself by being able to separate the two events. In her heart of hearts, she knew that Julie was right. She had fallen victim to a sexual predator, and it wasn't her fault. The bastard had violated her in the most egregious way, both physically and emotionally. It would take time, but she believed that eventually she would heal from the scars.

Diane suddenly heard footsteps behind her and turned around. The priest warmly shook hands with her. They exchanged greetings, and Diane thanked him for meeting with her. He said his office seemed stuffy today and suggested they go into the sanctuary to talk. They would be alone.

This was the moment that Father Bernard had been waiting for. The endless hours of speculation and wearing out his shoe leather was coming to an end. After Diane called to set up the appointment, he lifted up a quick prayer of thanks. Finally, his curiosity would be satisfied, and he was very confident that his priestly role would be reinstated in her life.

As they walked down the hardwood floors of the sanctuary to the altar, Diane could hear the echo of her heeled shoes. Father Bernard stopped and seated them in the front pew. Diane could smell the pungent odor of wood polish. As they sat facing each other, the priest gently took her hand and offered up a prayer. Diane didn't resist. She felt comforted by this gesture. Inviting God into their conversation seemed like a good idea to her. Father Bernard thought Diane would be more comfortable with the prayer and not hold back. He still felt a little guilty about eavesdropping on Diane and Julie's private conversation, but concluded that it was providential that he did so.

After some small talk, Diane started to open up about her feelings about her husband's affairs and the sexual assault. But then, they heard loud voices. Both of them were startled by the sudden intrusion into their private conversation. They turned around and stared at the back of the church.

"What in the world?" the priest said.

Instantly, the wooden doors to the sanctuary were flung open, and Jeff Fouts was standing there glaring at them. Mrs. Hansen was standing behind him. Diane turned around to get a better look and stood up. Father Bernard stood up as well. Fouts quickly made his way down the aisle and joined them in the front of the church. For a moment, they all just looked at one another.

"What do you want? Why are you here?" Diane asked in rapid succession. Her voice had a disgusting tone.

"I need to talk to you!" Fouts exclaimed.

"Right now? Can't you see I am talking to Father Bernard?"

"Right now!" he said in a high-pitched, demanding voice.

Diane apologized to the priest. Father Bernard thought it expedient to remove himself. He quickly retreated to the sacristy to the left of the altar, but kept the door open to see what was happening. Mrs. Hansen hastened back to her office and shut the door.

"Now, what is it that you want? What is so important that it couldn't wait?" she asked.

"Do you remember the gun I bought from Herbert Hager?" He was talking very fast.

Diane wrinkled her nose and furrowed her eyebrows. What gun? she thought. What is he talking about?

After a few moments hesitation, Fouts jumped in and reminded her that, when he brought the gun home, she had made a fuss and didn't want it in the house. She was afraid for the children's safety if they found it.

"Yes, I do remember, now that you mention it," she said. "What of it?"

Before he could answer, they heard doors slamming somewhere in the church. Suddenly, Sam and Sigenthaler came rushing into the sanctuary through the same door Fouts had entered. Fouts and Diane turned around and looked at the officers. Then Fouts repositioned himself so his wife was between him and the officers.

As they approached, Fouts broke into a cold sweat. When they were about ten feet away, the officers stopped. No one said anything. Sam looked at Fouts and said they needed to interview him at the police station. Fouts began to shake. Diane stared at him.

"What is going on, Jeff? Why are you shaking?" she asked.

Fouts immediately reached into the pocket of his suit coat and grabbed his gun. He pulled it out and pointed it at the two officers. Diane shrieked.

Both Sam and Sigenthaler instantly drew their weapons. The two officers pointed their guns at Fouts, and he pointed his gun at them. No one said anything. The atmosphere in the church was suddenly very tense and edgy. It was a standoff. The air was thick and tightly wound.

"Please, put the gun down," Sam pleaded. "We only want to ask you some questions about Dr. Buckle's murder."

Diane gasped!

Father Bernard was in shock. He had an overwhelming urge to rush out from his hiding spot to be of assistance. After all, they were in his church. He slowly made his way to the surreal group of people with guns drawn.

Fouts saw him and pointed his gun at Diane, and then he looked again at the priest. "Don't come any closer."

Father Bernard stopped.

"Okay." He spoke barely above a whisper.

Now there were five people involved. The life-and-death drama being played out in the church was dreamlike and bizarre.

As Fouts looked around the group one at a time, they all stared back at him. What was going to happen next? What was he going to do?

Fouts looked at the gun in his hand and looked perplexed. Then, suddenly and without warning, he pointed the gun at his own head. Sam and Diane simultaneously let out a loud scream! The others looked first at Diane and then to Sam. Sam instantly had a creepy haunting feeling of deja vu that sent shivers throughout her whole body.

Fouts lowered his gun. Father Bernard couldn't contain himself any longer and started to say something. Fouts turned and pointed the gun at him. "Shut up Priest! Damn you!" he shouted. Father Bernard felt faint and quickly sat down on the cool floor.

Throughout this madness, Diane's mind was racing as all the chaos unfolded around her. Her face contorted itself into a mask of disbelief. Then, unexpectedly, she had a moment of clarity. The dark emotional cloud that had been hovering over her started to clear. She took a step toward her husband. She felt a sense of empowerment. The gun Fouts was holding didn't frighten her. She looked Fouts straight in the eye. She had his full attention.

Sigenthaler was getting antsy. Sam touched his arm to calm him. She was terrified, because she had no idea how this was going to play out. Her instincts told her that shooting Fouts may be the only outcome to save lives.

"Did you kill Dr. Buckle?" Diane asked in a loud commanding voice that echoed through the church.

Fouts hesitated. The question hung in the air. He instantly knew his fate. He was trapped with no means of escape. He looked down at his shoes and then back to Diane. Diane's jaw was set, and she was grinding her teeth. Her laser-like stare bore a hole into his soul.

"I did it for you, Diane," he replied weakly. Diane exploded.

"How could you? You bastard! Don't lie to me! You didn't do it for me, and you know it!"

Fouts stopped breathing for an instant. The outburst from his wife surprised him and took him to another place. He had never seen his wife like this before. He didn't respond. He was in shock. For once in his life, he was speechless. Diane continued.

"Cat got your tongue, you jerk?" she said sarcastically. "You have lied to me during our entire marriage, and you are still lying to me. You lied about your affairs. Those damnable affairs destroyed me and our marriage. And all that crap you told me, that you weren't having affairs but just straying, makes me sick to my stomach! And now you have killed a doctor, for God's sake! You are sick Jeffery, you are sick!"

Sam and Sigenthaler stood by silently and at the ready as this heated verbal assault continued. Sam noticed that Fouts had lowered his arm, and his gun was now pointing at the floor. It was Sam's thought just to let it continue to play out. However, she was still prepared to use her weapon if it became necessary.

Fouts looked at Diane like a child who was being scolded by a parent.

"I love you, Diane," he pleaded. "That bastard raped you, and I had to do the right thing. I didn't think of it as right or wrong at the time. I was only giving him what he deserved. I did it for you. Can't you understand that?"

Diane threw her arms to the sky.

"What I understand is that you didn't do it for me, so don't try to lay that guilt at my feet. Killing the doctor was all for you. All those trips out west so you could live out some bizarre fantasy of frontier justice found its way into your psyche. Who do you think you are? John Wayne?" She paused and waited for a reply. The years of frustration and fear were quickly melting away. She could feel the adrenaline rush, and she savored the moment!

Fouts took his eyes off Diane and looked at his feet again. As she waited, the tears started flowing down her cheeks. The tears just kept coming and coming. She had stood her ground. She was determined. The exhilaration she felt as she confronted her husband was intoxicating. She had waited a long time for this! She spoke again.

"So here we are today. You are waving a gun around looking like some adolescent child. Who are you going to shoot next? The police officers, the priest, me, or how about yourself? Have you even thought about our children? What kind of legacy are you leaving them? If you shoot either me or yourself, you will change them forever." She paused for a moment and let this sink in. "If you love them, you will put down the gun."

The mention of the children further deflated him. He looked up at Diane's red, water-logged eyes. He raised his gun, and the two police officers tensed up. They still had their weapons pointed at him. Fouts looked around and saw the priest sitting on the floor praying. He looked at the two police officers holding their guns. Diane was staring at him as if looking at a stranger, showing no expression or fear.

He was a beaten man. He could hear the drum beat of defeat as the cadence pounded in his head. Fouts slowly bent over, placed the gun on the floor and backed up. His raised his hands up over his head. Sigenthaler quickly moved in and handcuffed him. Everyone watched silently as Sigenthaler led Fouts back up the aisle and out of the church to his pending fate. He offered no resistance. A big sigh of relief filled the church. Father Bernard immediately jumped up and looked for someone to hug. Sam put her arms around Diane and held her tightly.

EPILOGUE

Jeff Fouts confessed to the murder of Dr. George Andrew Buckle and is currently serving a life sentence in prison. Diane Fouts filed for divorce and is quietly getting on with her life and raising their children.

Dr. Ingrid Lindquist sold her house and moved back to Stockholm, Sweden, where she is enjoying a successful career working at the Karolinska University Hospital.

Detective Sam Gates and Drew Nelson rescheduled their long weekend in Galena, Illinois, and had a wonderful time together.

Dwayne Burkhalter healed from his injuries and borrowed $1,000 from his Uncle Harold. As he drove his pickup truck down the driveway of the farm, heading to Alaska, his mother watched and cried. In her heart she felt that he would be back someday and take over running the farm.

Father Bernard is back to normal. He is sleeping well and attending to the needs of his flock.

CPSIA information can be obtained at www.ICGtesting.com
Printed in the USA
LVOW122329200912

299616LV00002B/1/P